MIDNIGHT ON THE MIDWAY

CARNIVAL OF MYSTERIES

MORGAN BRICE

eBook ISBN: 978-1-64795-083-5
Print ISBN: 978-1-64795-084-2

Midnight on the Midway, Copyright © 2024 by Gail Z. Martin.
Cover Art by Diane Theis, LyricalLines.net
Editor: Misty Massey
The Carnival of Mysteries, Errante Ame, Madame Persephone, and Peter
the Potion Master © 2023 Ari McKay, used with permission.

Darkwind Press is an imprint of DreamSpinner Communications, LLC

CONTENTS

CHAPTER ONE

DRAKE

F BSI! Stop!" Drake Carlson shouted at the skinny man who raced for the nearest alley.

The man knocked a pile of garbage into Drake's path and kept running.

Drake pivoted and leaped, clearing the obstacle and staying on his quarry. He drew his gun and hoped he didn't have to shoot. Since he wasn't sure what kind of creature the man really was, Drake couldn't be certain a bullet would make a difference, and he didn't want to cause a scene in public if the perp decided to use magic or shift into an animal.

Skinny Guy put on a burst of speed, and Drake pushed himself to keep up. He hated foot chases. Unlike on television, they were dangerous and usually meant dodging rats and stinking dumpsters.

He's going to take a right—into a dead end. Drake's psychic abilities came in handy. He'd had a vision about this chase, and now he intentionally herded the guy toward where the back street was blocked.

Sure enough, the other end of the new street had been

closed off. Skinny Guy looked around wildly, then froze. His shape began to waver. Drake knew if the man shifted, he could lose him.

They were alone in the alley, with no one in sight in any direction. Drake stopped and aimed, firing a shot. It hit the man in the thigh and sent him crashing to the pavement. Drake's bullet incised with runes stopped him from changing shape. Drake was on him fast, cuffing him with silver handcuffs etched with magical symbols.

"Get off me!" The man struggled against Drake's height and weight advantage.

"FBSI," Drake told him. That extra letter stood for supernatural, the branch of the department that investigated crimes involving magic, non-human creatures, and anything paranormal. "You're under arrest."

"For what? I can walk down an alley if I want. It's a free country."

Drake patted him down and pulled a bag of powder from the man's pocket. "Walking? Yes. Dealing—no."

"It's flour. I picked it up for my dear old granny."

"Uh-huh. What flavor of 'monster meth' are you running? Shifter smack or vamp Valium?"

"What the fuck are you talking about monsters for?"

Drake's knee pressed a little harder into the small of the man's back. "Like you weren't trying to shift."

Skinny Guy quit fighting. The runes on the silver cuffs blocked any magic, and the silver kept him from changing shape. Blood trickled from his temple. "Look, man, I'm a nobody. I'm not worth the paperwork."

"True." Drake pretended to think about it and drew his gun. "It's less complicated if you're shot resisting arrest."

"Hey, hey, hey! Don't be hasty. Shooting me won't change anything."

"Maybe not. But it sends a message to your bosses that we're watching."

"They don't care. You can't touch them."

"Guess we'll find that out. Tell me what and who you know, and maybe we can work a deal."

"Okay, okay. Fuck, don't shoot me again. This job doesn't pay enough for that."

Drake called for backup. Before long, an FBSI van with two agents parked to block the entrance to the alley. Drake hauled the prisoner to his feet and perp-walked him to the vehicle, keeping a firm grip as the man staggered.

"Charge him for dealing and possession of paranormal pharmaceuticals. Hold him in a shifter cell and get one of our docs to look at him. I'll be in to question him once he's processed," Drake told them after flashing his badge. They took Skinny Guy away with little more than an acknowledgment.

He watched them drive away, dusted himself off, and swore when he noticed that tackling the suspect had gone hard on his favorite pair of jeans.

"Shit. That's the third pair this month."

Drake Carlson usually loved his job as a Special Agent with the Federal Bureau of Supernatural Investigation. The FBSI handled the same type of crimes as their mundane counterpart, but their focus involved anything to do with paranormal creatures, magic, witches, psychics, spirits, and the supernatural.

Trafficking illegal drugs specially formulated for the heightened metabolisms of shifters and vampires definitely fell under the agency's purview.

Drake had recently been assigned to a case in Moundsville investigating the local syndicate of mobsters dealing in paranormal drugs—all types, but especially zombie drugs that could be used to coerce the victim. His new partner, Clark Mullins, had driven to Charleston, the capital of West Virginia, to research the financial connections of the shifter drug cartel that had caused a dozen overdose deaths and plenty of turmoil as factions fought for control.

"He was right about the paperwork," Drake muttered as he headed to his car. They'd gotten tips that Moundsville had turned into the hot spot for the drug arm of the supernatural syndicate, but he needed details to open a full investigation. That meant poking around to see what he could find and hoping he'd get a lucky break.

He headed back to his hotel room and computer. Drake completed the required report and filed it, then sat back and finished his Coke. The FBSI wouldn't be through processing Skinny Guy until tomorrow, so interrogating him would have to wait.

Drake had recently transferred from the Beckley office after he had gotten on the wrong side of his supervisor by pursuing a case that angered some corrupt bigwigs. He had been afraid that he was going to need to leave the FBSI until a job opened up in Wheeling. Leaving the toxic office in Beckley felt like a rescue. Despite being assigned there for two years, Drake hadn't put down roots or made any real friends outside of work. Romantic options had been slim.

He hoped Wheeling would be better. Drake already liked his new boss and coworkers more than the Beckley crew. Moving and getting resettled had taken all of his attention and free time, but now that those tasks were over, Drake intended to put more effort into building a life outside the office—as much as an FBSI agent could.

The job demanded time and attention—and putting himself in danger. Drake loved his job, hated the paperwork, and enjoyed the research. Sometimes, between cases, hours were regular. In the middle of an investigation, days and nights blended together, and schedules were unpredictable.

When he was younger, Drake had rolled with the chaos, loving the excitement. Now, heading into his mid-thirties, he hoped he could find someone special and carve out something for himself beyond the badge.

That, however, was a project for another day.

Drake's leg jiggled beneath the desk, and he caught himself drumming his fingers.

Adrenaline coursed through his blood, making him twitchy from the fight. That meant settling in for a night of cable movies and pizza wasn't going to cut it.

Drake scrolled on his phone to see what kind of entertainment was nearby. The word arcade caught his eye, and he clicked on the image of a neon sign.

Games Galore And More was a high-tech destination that offered the newest arcade-style video games, Skee-Ball, pinball, bowling, escape rooms, a black light indoor mini-golf range, and billiards, as well as a full bar with an appealing snack menu.

That looked exactly like what Drake needed to blow off steam and work out the restlessness from the adrenaline surge. Even better, it was something he could do by himself that still felt social. Maybe he could find someone to play billiards or golf with once he was there. If he was really lucky, he might *get* lucky. Drake wasn't counting on that, but it was nice to think about. He drove his black Silverado, not planning to have more than one or two beers.

Games Galore was an arcade player's wet dream, playing up the fun with bright colors, neon, and strings of white bulb lights. Drake felt the day's tension and danger fade as he walked inside to the cacophony of music, bells, game noises, and the occasional grand prize siren.

This was a Wednesday night, so the place wasn't packed

like Drake had feared. He found a spot at the bar and ordered wings, fries, and a beer. Habit and training meant he checked his surroundings. No one looked out of place. One group of college-aged guys were having a good time with a deer-hunting video game. A few couples drifted from game to game, more interested in each other than in points or tickets.

At the end of the bar, Drake noticed a good-looking man eating a Reuben and watching strangers play their games. Since the man's attention was elsewhere, Drake took the opportunity to enjoy the view.

He guessed the stranger was early thirties, close to his age, give or take a few years. Short reddish blond hair and a slender-but-fit build appealed to Drake, although he hadn't really come to the arcade to cruise for a date. He wondered why the man was there by himself. Was he at loose ends, like Drake, wanting the company of a public meal? He didn't seem interested in the sporting events playing on the big screens over the bar and hadn't talked to anyone except the bartender.

Reluctantly, Drake tore his attention away from the stranger. He eyed the games and tried to decide what to do next.

Video racing was more fun with a partner. Drake was tolerably good at pinball—enough not to have the game end right away—and some of the new machines looked cool. He knew the basketball games were rigged by having a narrow hoop to make shots harder to sink, but he still usually had good luck.

The elaborate large-scale zombie hunt video games reminded Drake too much of his day job. Billiards, mini-golf, bowling, and the escape room weren't one-person games. Then he saw the pinball machines and Skee-Ball and grinned.

He paid for his meal and when he looked up, searching

for the server, he caught the cute stranger giving him the once-over. Amused and curious, Drake smiled but didn't make any move to attract the man or put him off.

Let's see what happens. Maybe I'll at least find someone to play a few games with.

The double entendre wasn't lost on him, although it had been a while since he had hooked up with someone.

First, he warmed up shooting hoops, missing more than he sank. He didn't care—he wasn't in it for the tickets, although he scooped them up when he finished.

Drake checked out the pinball machines next. He rarely hit high scores, but he loved how hands-on the game was and the fun of the lights and bells. It reminded him of the small, crowded, smoky arcade in his hometown, where he had spent a lot of his teenage years.

"You're pretty good."

Drake looked up when his game ended to see the blond guy from the bar leaning against the next machine.

"Thanks. I'm no wizard, but I get some extra rounds."

"Want to try some of the two-player games? That is if you're not here with someone…"

Drake smiled. "No, I'm not with anyone. And I'd love to try some of those games." He paused. "I'm Drake."

"Garrett," the other man said with a grin that made Drake's heart skip a beat. "Want to race?"

Drake braced for the younger man to be a cutthroat competitor and was pleasantly surprised when he was competent but not overly invested. That was a nice change from the dick-measuring overcompetitiveness that often went with playing against someone he didn't already know.

The arcade had several paired simulators where gamers could race against each other. Drake and Garrett started with the mountain bikes, zooming down a realistic video course that looked like somewhere out West. Drake won, but not by much, and happily agreed to a rematch.

From there, they moved on to the jet skis, and this time, Garrett eked out a win.

"Best two out of three?" Drake was happy to find their skills so evenly matched.

"You know it! Bring it on!" Garrett grinned.

The final course involved snowmobiles, mountain roads, and an unfortunate avalanche. Drake ceded gracefully to Garrett's win.

"That was fun." Garrett scooped up his tickets and slid them into his pocket. "Want to play something else?"

Garrett didn't question when Drake picked a deer-hunting two-player virtual reality game over the zombies. They tried a few more video games before Garrett nodded toward the mini-golf.

"I suck at mini-golf, but it's the thought that counts, right?" Garrett looked like he was having the time of his life. "Let's give it a try."

Drake couldn't claim to be a golf master, but at least he didn't embarrass himself by going over the number of strokes allotted for each hole. The black light made their clothing glow, which gave them both a good laugh.

"Someone really went all-out planning this." Garrett nodded toward the elaborate course. Not only were each of the holes laid out differently, but they all had some crazy additions to make the shots more challenging. Ape monsters, giant lizards, UFOs, and a tilted golf cart were just some of the obstacles hiding the holes. Everything glowed in the black light, giving the room a trippy feel.

"I haven't played in a long time—and it shows," Drake said ruefully as they tallied their scores.

"Neither have I. But it doesn't matter—that was fun. I wonder how you get the job of making these things up?"

Garrett asked as they left the course and turned in their clubs.

"I don't know, but it's got to beat most nine-to-fives," Drake agreed. "How are you at Skee-Ball?"

"I thought you'd never ask." Garrett's broad grin gave him dimples and made his hazel eyes sparkle. Drake couldn't help noticing. He hadn't come looking to get laid, but he wouldn't turn it down if Garrett offered.

Through a dozen rounds of Skee-Ball, they teased each other goodnaturedly, double-dared one another to hit specific scores, and talked trash like teenagers. Drake ended up with the high score, although he offered to split the tickets with Garrett.

"No way, man. They're yours fair and square. I don't want to come between you and one of those *awesome* prizes." Garrett winked.

Drake had taken a peek at the rewards room on the way in. The high-end electronic prizes were definitely over-priced if anyone did the math on how many games it would take to accumulate enough tickets. On the lower end, cheesy prizes like bobbleheads, foam darts, stuffed animals, and glowsticks still appealed to his memories of childhood.

"Want to try an escape room?" Garrett asked when they finished Skee-Ball. "They have five different themes, and they all look fun."

"Have you ever done one before?" Drake asked, dubious.

"Once or twice. It's not really locked—you can get out if you feel trapped or need to pee," Garrett assured him. "You have to find the clues to solve the mystery, and you have an hour to do it."

"Sounds fun. What kind of themes?" Drake knew nothing about the rooms, so he was glad to let Garrett take the lead.

"There's a space one and a haunted house, as well as an

ancient temple, an old mine, and something that looks like Alcatraz," Garrett read from his phone.

"Do you have a preference?"

"Haunted house? If that's okay with you." Garrett's enthusiasm made Drake smile.

"Fine with me. I like that kind of thing." Understatement of the year. *Just remember, everything is fake. Don't salt and burn anything, and don't stake the actors.*

The attendant opened the door to the game set and went over the rules. "There are multiple rooms that are all part of the adventure. I'm not going to tell you how many because finding them is half the fun. You can move objects that reposition easily, but please don't damage the pieces or break anything. Nothing requires putting holes in the walls, tearing away the wallpaper, or removing anything that is fastened in place."

Clearly, some players had gotten over-invested, Drake thought.

"Relax, be creative, and have fun," the man went on. Drake could guess his thoughts as he glanced at him and Garrett. "And remember—you're on camera!"

Garrett blushed, which told Drake that his new friend had considered similar alternatives to what had occurred to him. The longer they were together, the more Drake thought the odds of the evening having a happy ending increased.

Garrett hadn't said anything overt, but there had been plenty of innocent shoulder bumps, elbow checks, and the brush of a hand against his—all plausibly deniable but not accidental.

Drake knew it was an occupational hazard to wonder if hitting it off so quickly was really a honey trap set up by the syndicate to discredit or even kill him. His psychic ability wasn't picking up danger signals or magic, which helped to decrease the odds of mere human treachery.

Earlier, he had "accidentally" spilled his soda on their hands. That gave him the excuse to offer napkins and a pocket-sized bottle of hand sanitizer, which Garrett had gratefully accepted. The cleanser was laced with holy water, salt, and colloidal silver. Garrett didn't combust or break out into a nasty rash, ruling out most supernatural creatures.

For now, Drake was willing to accept a turn of good luck at face value.

The attendant left the room which was designed to look like a Victorian parlor, and they heard the door click shut behind him. Ominous music began to play, and after a few minutes, Drake picked up other sounds like chattering teeth, moans, and wails.

"They go all-out, don't they?" He followed Garrett's lead to handle the objects on shelves and tables, gently shifting them to disclose secrets.

"This place has a good reputation." Garrett turned slowly to survey the room.

Drake resisted the temptation to dive in with his agent training and decided to let Garrett take the lead. "I've never done one of these. Where do we start?"

Garrett looked pleased to share his love of the adventures. "This one was rated spooky but not extreme. It's not like one of those live haunted houses at the beach where actors follow you around and chase you. Some places do have characters, but this one doesn't."

"Have you done it before?"

Garrett shook his head. "Not this particular scenario. I did the UFO one here a couple of weeks ago with some friends from work. So I'm basing my expectations on that."

"So we get to live out our inner Scooby-Doo?"

"Pretty much. Trap doors may open, but you won't fall through anything. Handle anything that's loose and look for clues or codes. Gently tug on things to see if they move. If it opens, look inside. There will be doors to other rooms, so look for hidden openings as well as regular doors," Garrett said. "It's more fun if we work together, so don't try to do it all on your own."

Drake thought that working together on a project might feel awkward, or there could be a push-pull vying to be in charge. To his relief, Garrett proved to be competent and inquisitive without any one-upmanship.

They divided the room into search sections, moving clockwise so they eventually went over each other's areas without getting in the way. Garrett found the first of several clues and seemed genuinely pleased when Drake found a secret door that opened to lead them into a long-abandoned dining room.

A sudden shriek raised the hackles on Drake's neck. Garrett chuckled. "Gotta watch out for the sound effects. They'll get you every time."

Drake relaxed, chagrined, and reminded himself that this wasn't the usual life-or-death stakes. As he searched behind paintings, checked under couch cushions, and peered inside the grandfather clock, Drake admired the clever set dressing and the ingenuity of the scriptwriter.

Real ghost hunts rarely went smoothly, and while the escape room was made to look like a creepy abandoned house, it lacked the smell of mildew, rodents, and disuse that came with the real thing.

"You're pretty good at this." Garrett bumped elbows with Drake. "I think you've got a knack for it."

If you only knew.

They finished scouring the parlor and moved through the secret door into the dining room, where they started the search again.

Drake and Garrett had barely separated when a gray

apparition blinked into view just behind where Garrett stood.

Without thinking, Drake pushed Garrett behind him and stepped forward, with his hand going to the folding knife in his pocket.

"Remember—it's all pretend," Garrett warned.

The ghost blinked out. Drake scanned the crown molding around the ceiling for the location of a projector. His reactions didn't know this was a game, and he felt his heart rate spike.

"Um, thanks for protecting me." Garrett looked at Drake with bemusement and curiosity. "You've got really good reflexes."

"Can't go losing a good gaming partner, can I?" Drake laughed it off. The look in Garrett's eyes told him the man was trying to figure him out as much or more than he was the game.

Over the next three rooms, Drake and Garrett fell into a comfortable rhythm searching for clues and comparing notes. Drake managed to tune out the sound effects and tone down his reaction the next time a projected ghost appeared right in front of him.

Thanks to Garrett's experience with other escape challenges and Drake's on-the-job observation and deduction skills, they beat the room in less than an hour. The host awarded prize tickets to both of them and reminded them to cash out soon since it was nearly closing time.

"That was a blast!" Garrett looked happy and flushed with success as they walked over to the rewards center to get their prizes. "I bet we could beat the other rooms if we tried."

Drake felt suddenly warm at the idea that there could be a next time.

"That sounds like fun." He met Garrett's gaze and saw what he hoped was similar interest. "After all, we haven't bowled or played billiards yet—and we missed a couple of the video games."

They stopped to exchange tickets on the way out. Drake opted for a Magic 8 Ball and a dart game. Garrett went for candy and several flying disks, still joking and laughing as they made their picks.

The lights flashed, warning everyone that the arcade was about to close. Drake and Garrett walked out together to the dark and nearly empty parking lot.

"Where are you parked? I can drive you over," Drake offered.

"I'd appreciate that. I'm at the other end." Even with the tall security lights, the lot was a little creepy.

Drake gestured toward his truck. "I'm happy to give you a ride."

Garrett's smile turned coy. "I'd appreciate that."

Drake knew he hadn't missed the innuendo in Garrett's tone. He was certain when they reached his truck, and Garrett stepped closer and met his gaze.

"I had a really good time tonight." He reached out and let his fingers trace down Drake's arm. "Just because the arcade closed, we don't have to go home."

Drake had been half hard most of the night, reacting to Garrett. It had been a long time since Drake's last hook-up, and he hoped Garrett might be more than a one-night stand.

"There's plenty of room in the crew cab," Drake said in a low, husky voice. He nodded toward his truck. "Tinted windows, too."

He had no desire to get busted by mall security, but he had parked close enough to the movie theater that his truck wouldn't seem odd while also sitting apart from the other cars.

Garrett's sly grin held a world of promise, and his hand slid down to take Drake's. "Let's go."

They piled into the back seat of the truck, fumbling and touching everywhere. It had been a while for Drake, and he felt as awkward as a teenager. Fortunately, Garrett didn't seem to mind.

Garrett leaned in to kiss him, and his hands slid down the front of Drake's shirt, stopping to stroke and tweak his nipples.

"No marks," Drake managed.

"Fine by me—this time."

"Can I touch you?" Drake almost didn't recognize his own voice, rough and lower than usual.

"I was counting on it."

Drake struggled with Garrett's belt as Garrett returned the favor. He reached for the bottle of hand lotion in the divider between the front seats and slicked up his hand, freed Garrett's hard cock from his briefs, then his own.

"This okay?" he growled.

"Definitely okay." Garrett seemed fine with Drake taking the lead.

Their cocks were too thick for Drake to completely wrap his hand around them, but Garrett added his, and the friction was perfect.

"Oh, yeah. Just like that," Garrett moaned as they got the rhythm right. Garrett mouthed at Drake's throat but didn't suck a hickey or bite. Still, the feel of his lips and tongue got Drake hard and too close too fast.

"Not going to last," Drake breathed. "Been a while."

"Same," Garrett breathed. "We'll have to do something about that."

They thrust into the channel of their hands, hard and slick, leaking pre-come. "Come on," Garrett coaxed in a sinful growl. "Show me what you can do."

That pushed Drake over the edge. His whole body stiffened, and he arched as his cock spurted his release over their joined hands. Garrett followed seconds later, gasping and beautiful and completely open.

Drake reached up front and grabbed fast food napkins from the glove compartment to clean them up, then handed Garrett a bottle of sanitizer to clean the rest off their hands.

"That was—"

"Yeah," Garrett agreed as they tucked themselves back in, zipped and buckled. "It was."

For a moment, they stared at each other like teenagers who had gotten away with something before bursting into laughter. Drake was surprised that the aftermath felt comfortable and not weird.

"How about I drive you over to where you're parked, and you give me your phone number?" Drake said after he had checked to make sure they didn't crawl out of the back of his truck right in front of mall security.

"I'd like that."

They got into the front seats, and Drake followed Garrett's instructions to a dark green Chevy Suburban. "This yours?"

Garrett nodded. "Yep. She's got a lot of miles on her, but she hasn't let me down yet." He pulled out his phone. "What's your number?"

Drake gave it to him, and Garrett sent a text. "There. Now you've got mine too." He turned to look at Drake and laid a hand on his thigh.

"I really would like to see you again. After all, we never got to do bowling and billiards," Garrett added with a lazy smile. "And maybe next time, you can come back to my place —if you want. For some other entertainment."

"That sounds good. Real good." Drake was surprised at how much he wanted to see Garrett again. Aside from a hot hand job, he enjoyed Garrett's sense of humor, and something about the other man made him feel comfortable. Part of that was his psychic side cluing in to check for threats and not finding any, and the rest was pure sexual chemistry.

Garrett leaned in and gave him a peck on the cheek. "For luck," He gave a wink before he climbed out of the cab and swaggered a little on the walk over to his SUV.

Drake waited to make sure Garrett's truck started before heading in the opposite direction, squelching the desire to follow him home to make sure he got in okay.

That was...unexpectedly awesome. Drake tried to remember the last time he'd been with someone and realized it was long enough ago he remembered the circumstances—a bar in Nashville—but couldn't place the date.

It had been even longer since he'd had a real boyfriend. Despite the so-called glamor of being a federal agent, his job was more of a hindrance than an aphrodisiac. If he was on assignment, he usually didn't mingle, although tonight was an exception.

Back in Wheeling, Drake still had to be cautious. West Virginia wasn't New York when it came to accepting the LGBTQ community. His boss knew Drake was gay, but while he didn't keep it a secret, he also didn't see a need to bring it up in most situations. Drake was well aware there would be plenty of people—inside the bureau and outside—who didn't approve.

Hell, he'd even been taunted by a homophobic ghost.

Still, Drake had resolved not to hide. If Wheeling couldn't handle it, then it would be a pitstop and not a destination.

Now that he had met Garrett, he hoped this posting would work out. Moundsville wasn't far from Wheeling, so if this turned into something between them, commuting wouldn't be a problem. Drake wondered what Garrett did for a living and whether their schedules could work out.

Getting the cart in front of the horse a little, he chided himself.

A couple of years ago, Drake had fallen for an EMT. It was a running joke that in law enforcement, the hours and the nature of the job tended to mean finding a partner who worked similar schedules, which generally meant a first responder.

The chemistry had been great, and the sex was hot, but trying to see each other around Dan's chaotic on-call hours and Drake's assignments had finally proven too much.

A partner with a regular day job often grew to resent an agent's frequent travel, long hours, and dangerous work. Matching up with another agent was a recipe for disaster. There was a reason for the stereotype of agents being divorced and lonely in their off-hours.

Early in his career, settling down hadn't been high on Drake's priorities. He loved the constant change, the thrill of the hunt, the battle of wits, and the high of cheating danger.

After seeing his friends Bart and RJ, who worked with the Tennessee Bureau of Supernatural Investigation, hit it off, Drake had started to wonder whether finding a partner of his own might be in the cards.

Curb your enthusiasm, he warned himself. *One great not-date and a make-out session don't mean you've found the one.*

But wouldn't it be nice if it did?

CHAPTER TWO

GARRETT

*D*r. Garrett Thompson hummed as he poured another cup of coffee, still thinking about the night before and the hot stranger from the arcade.

Despite the late night, he had been up at six to open the clinic at seven. His first patient, a temperamental Yorkie, seemed vexed not to be able to rip him limb from limb.

After escaping without serious bloodshed, he deduced that the Yorkie had digestive issues—enough to make anyone grumpy—and prescribed an antacid and change of food. The grateful owner thanked him profusely, while Kong, the Yorkie, had given him a look that promised retribution.

"I think Kong was a German shepherd in his last life." Kirsten, his senior vet tech, said as she edged in to get coffee for herself. "He probably remembers, and he's pissy because he got demoted."

Garrett laughed. "Maybe you're right. Although I've met plenty of shepherds who don't have that big of a chip on their shoulder." The creative tales Kirsten spun about their patients kept the whole staff entertained, giving their patients elaborate backstories and motivations.

Kirsten cocked her head as she looked at him. "You're in a good mood."

"I'm always in a good mood."

She snorted. "Doc, you are *not* a morning person. Everyone knows that."

"Maybe I got a good night's sleep."

"Uh-uh. You're on your third cup of coffee earlier than usual. Do something fun yesterday?"

Garrett gave an elaborate sigh. "Busted. I binge-watched the latest season of that new monster hunter show. Finally got all caught up." He hated to lie, but Garrett made it a point not to mix business and personal at the clinic. His staff knew he was gay and single, but they didn't need to know the ups and downs of his love life. Which, to be honest, had been more down than up before last night.

His most recent serious relationship lasted two years and broke down because his boyfriend didn't like the long hours that running the veterinarian clinic required. The city had both urgent care and emergency care options that picked up the tough cases, so Garrett's office wasn't as swamped as it could be.

Still, caring for his furry patients meant catering to the realities of their human parents, and that meant office hours that allowed drop-off and pick-up before and after normal working hours, weekends, and some evenings. The clinic did well, but while Garrett would have loved to hire a second vet to share the load, the budget wouldn't stretch for more than the main clinic staff, vacation coverage for him to take a couple of weeks off, and a vet who only worked Saturdays to help cover the busiest times.

Garrett sighed. The business side was his least favorite part of running the clinic. His true love lay in helping dogs, cats, and the occasional guinea pig or chinchilla feel better and navigate their health problems.

Kirsten's eyes narrowed as she watched him. "You look more relaxed than usual."

"You say that like it's a bad thing," Garrett quipped.

"You're never relaxed."

"Not true. I was in a really good mood after Christmas break."

Kirsten rolled her eyes. "That lasted until the Barton's cocker spaniel tried to bite your nose."

"And nearly succeeded," Garrett pointed out with feigned indignance. "He's a killer underneath all that cuteness."

"No doubt," she said dryly. "But the point remains— you're suspiciously bouncy. Spill."

"Can't a guy just be in a good mood?"

"You have two moods—on-duty and asleep," she replied. "I've seen you doze on your desk more than once. Did you actually do something fun?"

Garrett didn't mind Kirsten's good-natured questions. She was the same age as his older sister, and he knew she didn't mean anything by her inquiries except for genuinely wanting him to be happy.

"I went back to that fancy arcade place. The food was just as good, and I hung around and played games for a while," he admitted.

"By yourself?" Kirsten raised an eyebrow.

"I'll have you know I'm a bona fide adult who can go places alone," he joked.

"Never said you weren't. But most people go to an arcade with friends or a date."

"I got into some pick-up games with people who were there. It was fun."

"Pick-up as in spontaneous, or as in *pick-up*?" Kirsten generally saw right through Garrett's deflections.

"I plead the fifth."

"Hmm. The absence of a denial is the same as admitting the presence of something," she teased.

"You missed your calling as a prosecuting attorney," Garrett replied. "Guilty as charged. I had fun playing mini-golf and escape room with a cute stranger. Not exactly stuff for the scandal page."

"Good for you." Kirsten had dropped the joking tone. "You need to get out more. Bailey's company, but sometimes you need more." She leaned down to pet Bailey as the black Labrador mix wound between their legs, hoping for treats.

"Don't listen to her, Bailey. You're my forever dog," Garrett joked to lighten the mood.

Bailey gave him a soulful look and went back to sniffing Kirsten's hand, where he found a treat.

Garrett had adopted Bailey after the dog's owner had to give him up because her child had developed severe animal dander allergies. Bailey was a sweetheart, and he served as the clinic's mascot and volunteer therapy dog, helping nervous owners and befriending patients.

"I'd forgotten how much I enjoyed playing those games." Garrett was happy to shift the topic. "There was an arcade at the mall in my hometown, and my friends and I spent a lot of time and money there. Even so, I somehow almost never made high score. It's the enthusiasm that counts, right?"

"I remember those mall arcades," Kirsten said. "They smelled like Axe and desperation."

Garrett laughed. "That's truer than you'll ever know." He set his coffee cup aside with a sigh. "I think this is going to be a three-pot day. Got a lot on the schedule."

"I already checked on the boarders—the kennel staff gave meds and was working on breakfasts. Patty and the front desk folks looked like they had everything under control. So that just leaves the appointments. You've got this, Doc."

Garrett smiled, appreciating the vote of confidence. "That's because I've got awesome staff."

The appreciation was wholehearted. Garrett hired good people and paid as well as he could afford. That meant low turnover, and people cared about their patients as much as he did. Most of his staff had been with him since he opened the clinic three years ago, buying out the practice from a vet who retired to the Bahamas.

Kirsten went back to the kennels, and Garrett checked his schedule. "Five minutes left. Plenty of time for coffee," he told Bailey and reached down to ruffle the dog's ears. "Who's a good boy? You know you are." The rush of warm affection he felt made him smile.

Everyone praised Garrett for his amazing rapport with animals. He always deflected the comments, saying that he must have a trustworthy face that made his patients more relaxed.

The reality was a little more unusual. While he couldn't actually talk to the animals like the fictional Dr. Doolittle, Garrett could read the emotions of animals instead of relying solely on their physical clues. He figured it must go at least a little bit both ways, because he had an uncanny knack for setting skittish patients at ease and helping aggressive animals calm down.

Kirsten stuck her head in the break room. "Your next appointment is here. It's Reginald."

Garrett grinned. "Reggie's a good dog."

"All dogs are good dogs," Kirsten replied. "I'll take Bailey in the back and send Eddie in to help. Reggie is in room C."

Garrett finished his coffee, washed his cup, and set it aside before heading through the back hall to the treatment room.

Reginald the Great Dane sat at attention with his owner,

Maxine. His black and white coloring always made him look like he was formally attired.

"How's everyone today?" Garrett greeted them with a smile for the owner and a barrage of happy thoughts for Reggie. He noticed that the big dog favored his right front foot.

"I think Reggie stepped on a splinter," Maxine said. "You know how touchy he is about his paws. He won't let me look."

Garrett made eye contact with Reggie, who quickly looked away. Definitely shifty.

"Will you let me look at your paw?" He sent plenty of good vibes, then stopped, trying to listen. He got a sense of pain and nervousness. Eddie slipped into the room, and Reggie looked between them nervously.

Given Reggie's size, they were in the treatment room with a table that raised and lowered so no one had to wrestle one hundred and fifty pounds of a four and a half foot dog onto the examination surface.

Reggie climbed on like a trouper, but Garrett and Eddie knew they weren't out of the woods yet.

"That's a very good dog." Garrett ran a hand down Reggie's neck and gave him a skritch behind the ears. "Down." Reggie obligingly lay down, upright.

"Now, let's have a look at that paw." Garrett shot a look at Eddie, who moved into position.

As soon as Garrett took Reggie's paw and started to examine it, the dog whined in distress and keeled over in a dead faint.

"I'm so sorry. He's always been like this," Maxine fretted. "I don't think it's an act."

"That's okay. Eddie's here to keep him steady while I get a look at that splinter."

Reggie was famous for his fainting spells. He didn't like getting shots, having his nails trimmed, his ears cleaned, or his teeth brushed. Most of the time, Garrett knew it was anxiety-triggered, but he felt quite certain that Reggie had learned to fake an episode to try to get out of something he didn't like.

"Yep, that's a splinter, but it's not in too deep," he told Maxine after checking the sore paw. "I'm going to pull it out, clean the wound, and wrap it up. Try to keep it dry and clean for at least a day."

If Reggie had been faking before, he was out when Garrett gently pulled the splinter from the paw pad with tweezers. Eddie made sure Reggie didn't suddenly scramble to his feet if he woke up and ensured he wouldn't bonelessly slip from the table. By the time Reggie lifted his head with a groggy look, the paw had been treated and bandaged. Garrett reached into his pocket and offered Reggie a treat, which he gobbled up without hesitation.

"He'll be fine," Garrett assured Maxine. "Try to keep him from walking or running more than necessary for the next day or two so it can heal, and check the area where he got the splinter to make sure there aren't more."

"You're always so good with him," Maxine gushed as Eddie lowered the table. Reggie gave her a pitiable look and an exaggerated limp.

"Don't let him fool you," Garrett warned with a smile. "While I'm sure his paw is sore, he's turning in an Oscar-worthy performance right now for maximum treats."

"Oh, I know. He's a total drama dog." Maxine bent over to kiss the top of Reggie's head. "He'd have me carrying him out to the car if he thought I could lift him."

The rest of the morning passed without incident. Garrett gave vaccinations, rechecked vitals on older dogs with ongoing health issues, did a wellness exam for an adorable beagle puppy, and wrote a prescription for a carsick chihuahua.

At lunch, he checked his phone. A text message stood out.

Drake: *Having a good day?*

Garrett tried not to think about how his heartbeat sped up like a schoolyard crush.

Garrett: *Pretty good so far. You?*

Drake: *Thinking about bowling and billiards.*

Garrett: *Me, too.*

Drake: *I can't do tonight. Want to meet up there tomorrow night for dinner and diversions?*

Garrett's mind provided all sorts of images for diversions.

Garrett: Sounds good to me.

The message put a spring in his step. Garrett adjusted his scrubs so his semi wasn't apparent. He hadn't been sure whether Drake would go for a second date. He liked Drake and got generally good vibes. While his sixth sense didn't work as well on humans as it did on animals, Garrett picked up something hidden or at least obscured about his new crush and wondered whether that was something to worry about.

It's only the second date. Of course there are all kinds of things we don't know about each other. I need to chill out and let it run its course.

Garrett joined in with the staff's delivery order of sub sandwiches for lunch and enjoyed the banter around the break room table as they ate. An over-enthusiastic golden retriever had pulled the groomer into the tub with him, and two boarding puppies in the exercise yard had bonded so much that they whined to each other when they returned to their kennels. The staff laughed and joked, recounting favorite exploits of their long-time patients.

That afternoon, Garrett had a couple of minor surgeries

and then more checkups. He breathed a sigh of relief at the end of his schedule when Kirsten found him.

"We've got a last-minute appointment." Kirsten's apologetic tone let him know she understood that he had been wrapping up. "New patient—Mr. Colletta—says the dog fell off a patio and might have bruised ribs."

Garrett picked up a jangled vibe that wasn't usual for Kirsten. "But…"

She shrugged. "I don't know. I just have a weird feeling, but there's nothing to confirm it."

"You think he hurt the dog?"

"No. He's super protective and very worried. But he might know who did. I'm just not sure his story is the whole truth."

Garrett figured he would know soon enough from the dog's energy. "Okay, let's go. We'll deal with whatever it is, and if it's a bad fit, we'll give him a referral to someone else for follow-up."

He had never seen Kirsten react to a patient's owner like that before. Garrett resolved to keep an open mind. Every pet deserved good care even if they had crappy pet parents.

"I'm Doctor Thompson," Garrett introduced himself when he entered the treatment room. "What seems to be the matter?"

A man in his late thirties sat on the bench next to a large gray and black boxer. The dog looked dangerous but gave Garrett a nonthreatening mix of love, loyalty, and anxiety vibes. He didn't seem to be afraid of the man; instead, Garrett picked up a sense of bonding that was unusually strong.

The man, on the other hand, set off all Garrett's alarms. Colletta wore expensive leisurewear, a top-brand hoodie, and track pants over pricey running shoes, and his haircut was more New York than Nashville. If central casting had served up a mafia enforcer, this guy would have nailed the part.

"Brian fell off the deck, and I'm afraid he hurt his ribs," Colletta said in a low growl that reinforced Garrett's initial impression.

"What symptoms make you think that?" Garrett resolved to take care of Brian and then make a referral. The owner gave Garrett a very bad feeling.

"He seemed winded when it happened, he didn't get up right away, and he didn't want to be touched on his side. I was afraid maybe he broke a rib or couldn't breathe right, you know?"

Despite his tough appearance and the menacing vibes he put off, Colletta seemed deeply and legitimately concerned. That bought him back a little credit in Garrett's book.

"I'd like to examine him. Does he bite?"

"Not unless I tell him to."

So much for winning me over. Still, every sick or injured animal deserved treatment, even if their owners were assholes.

"Hey, Brian. Are you going to let me have a look at you?" Garrett nodded to Kirsten, and she lowered the treatment table again.

Brian looked to his owner, who gave a nod and pointed. Brian walked over, and Garrett heard the owner give a quiet command that had the dog hopping onto the table and remaining still as it rose. Just from the few steps Brian took, Garrett agreed that something was wrong.

Garrett did his best to project comfort and safety to Brian as he approached the dog. "I need to touch the ribs gently to see if they're bruised or broken," he said aloud, as much for Brian's sake as for the owner.

Brian stood and permitted Garrett to run his hands

lightly over both sides of the rib cage, wincing when his fingers reached a certain spot.

"I'd like to do an X-ray to make sure we know what we're dealing with. Do you give permission?"

The man gave him a grumpy look and waved his hand. "Do what you need to do."

Garrett and Eddie took Brian to the back, and Garrett was relieved when the dog followed happily and stood still for the camera. He was further relieved when the scan showed that the bones were intact.

"The good news is, nothing's broken." Garrett posted the X-ray for Colletta to see. "That means there's no risk of puncturing a lung. But he's clearly still in pain from the bruising. The ribs should heal on their own in about six weeks. Until then, he should be kept as quiet as possible to speed healing. No running or tussling with other dogs."

"Can't you wrap them or something?" Colletta gave Garrett an appraising look like he doubted his qualifications.

"I'll give you a prescription for pain, which should make him comfortable. We don't recommend wrapping ribs in people or animals anymore because it makes for shallow breathing, and that can lead to pneumonia or a collapsed lung," Garrett said.

"I've had my ribs wrapped and didn't die," Colletta challenged. Garrett's inner sense was pinging an alarm. While he believed the stranger's concern for the dog was genuine, he picked up on violence that Garrett felt certain wasn't his imagination.

"It used to be common practice," Garrett agreed, not wanting to challenge the man. "But we've learned that constricting the chest can lead to worse problems. The medication and staying quiet should make him comfortable and that speeds healing. Just keep him from tussling or doing anything strenuous like leaping or jumping."

"He'd better be okay."

Garrett picked up on the implied threat. He bristled but didn't want to tangle with the man. "I believe he will be." Garrett forced himself to smile and focused on the dog. "Brian is a very good dog, aren't you?" He scratched the pooch behind the ears.

Despite his discomfort, Brian seemed happy, which eased Garrett's worry that the owner had caused the injury. While he couldn't read Brian's mind, his connection to his owner seemed unusually strong, even for a dog.

"Thank you." Colletta stood and reached for Brian's leash.

"They'll take care of everything at the front desk," Garrett breathed a sigh of relief when Colletta and the dog left the room.

"Everything go okay?" Kirsten asked when Garrett walked into the back.

"Yeah, although I'm okay with not having him as a repeat customer," Garrett admitted. "The dog is fine. He can stay," he joked.

Kirsten shuddered. "I agree. Something about that guy gave me the creeps."

Garrett spent the next hour in his office with Bailey asleep on his dog bed while the staff cleaned and shut down for the evening. Garrett was careful to leave with the others. He often worked late, but tonight he felt better being in a group. Bailey wagged, and Garrett didn't need to be psychic to know he wanted dinner.

"Well that was quite a day, wasn't it, Bailey?" he said as they drove. "I wish you could tell me what you thought of that last customer."

Bailey hadn't seen Colletta, so Garrett knew he wasn't going to get an answer.

When he got back to the house he rented, Garrett turned Bailey loose in the fenced backyard. Despite being at the clinic all day, Bailey still had energy to burn off. He ran zoomies from one side to the other, then thoroughly sniffed the bushes for squirrels and birds.

"Come on, I'm hungry." Garrett ushered them both back inside. He had a ham and potato casserole already prepped and set the oven to heat, then went to change.

His scrubs went in the laundry. Garrett grabbed an old pair of jeans and a comfortable T-shirt, then padded out to put dinner in the oven and feed Bailey.

When his phone dinged, Garrett felt a rush of pleased surprise to find a message.

Drake: *Working late. Getting delivery—again. What are you eating?*

Garrett thought of several risqué ways to answer that question but didn't feel secure enough yet to share them.

Garrett: *I made a casserole. What did you order?*

Drake: *Sounds good. I got a Philly cheesesteak. Hard to screw up.*

Garrett: *Still on for tomorrow?*

Garrett found himself holding his breath.

Drake: *Counting on it. See you soon. Sweet dreams.*

Garrett didn't usually get swoopy about new partners. He readily admitted now, looking back, that too many had been picked on combustibility instead of compatibility. Nothing wrong with having both, but in hindsight, he suspected that lust alone didn't last as long as shared interests outside the bedroom.

I'm getting ahead of myself. We've had one almost date. We're going back to play billiards and bowling—and I hope, take things further than before. But I really don't know him at all yet.

Although I'd like to.

Garrett's dream to become a veterinarian had propelled him through high school advanced placement and honors courses through college and vet school. He had been

31

prepared for long days and all-nighters. When he graduated, he signed on as an assistant vet with an established practice and saved his money to open his own office.

Buying the older doctor's building and client list had been like catching a tiger by the tail. Garrett had learned the hard way what he didn't know about running a practice, managing staff, and having money left over at the end of the month. At first, he slept in his office to reduce costs.

Finally, business picked up, and Garrett got an apartment and adopted Bailey. He enjoyed the work and liked his staff, but up to this point his schedule didn't lend itself to having the time to do a relationship right. Since he wasn't big on one-night stands, that meant watching a lot of movies with Bailey and jerking off when he got lonely.

And now there was Drake. Garrett knew their relationship was still new, but he was cautiously optimistic that they could be something special together. He didn't hide being gay, but he didn't flaunt his orientation, especially not in West Virginia, where the cities and the small towns could be a century apart in their opinions.

Could we be more than a couple of dates and a hop in the sack? Am I ready for something more?

Garrett had been single-minded in his quest to become a veterinarian. He didn't come from a wealthy family, and his father had been even less inclined to help with school costs when Garrett had been outed as a teen. That meant working his way through college and vet school, which didn't leave much time for socializing.

Ambition mixed with the need to show his father that he could succeed. He won scholarships and earned work-study programs. Other than some backseat or back room fumbling around, he had shelved his personal life to make it through school and build a practice.

Now Garrett wanted more. The clinic was finally operating in the black, although he certainly wasn't getting wealthy. Much as Garrett loved quiet nights at home with Bailey, he wanted to make up for lost time with friendships outside the office and a life partner he could love.

The timer dinged, and Garrett went to get his dinner out of the oven. He watched funny videos on his phone while he ate, then cleaned up the kitchen, fed Bailey, and moved into the living room.

Garrett felt too antsy to read, so he flipped channels until he found reruns of a favorite show, an action-adventure series about monster hunters. After demanding a short walk, Bailey curled up in his favorite chair and fell asleep, leaving the couch for Garrett.

He settled in with a glass of wine and some cheese, a slightly more grown-up version of watching television with popcorn and a soda as a kid. His mind wandered, thinking about his encounter with Drake, daydreaming about seeing him again.

Drake had been polite and approachable but also flirty and fun. He didn't pout when Garrett got a higher score and seemed honestly happy when Garrett won a round. Drake had been comfortable with small talk, and didn't try to escalate the evening too far, too fast. Even when they joked and trash-talked at the arcade, Drake hadn't been mean-spirited, and none of his comments felt barbed.

On top of that, he was handsome and hot as hell.

Drake hadn't said much about what he did for a living. He seemed comfortable around people and down-to-earth, not overly worried about spending money as they worked their way around the arcade. He wondered what had brought Drake to town and whether his business required a lot of travel.

Although it was far too soon to fantasize after only one date, Garrett hoped that Drake didn't have to be away from home a lot. His schedule was so busy, Garrett pictured settling down with someone who had a more regular job with predictable hours.

Then again, I guess we could get a house cleaner and a dog walker.

He caught himself and laughed at jumping so far ahead after only just meeting, but deep down, Garrett hoped that he would see a lot more of Drake—both date-wise and in bed.

Time to get my life together and see if I can find the one. Bailey needs a two-parent family.

Full and happy with wine and dinner, Garrett slouched, daydreaming more than he was paying attention to the show. He thought about Drake in everyday situations around the house—running errands, cleaning up, cooking dinner, or working in the yard.

That last task conjured up images of Drake shirtless, glistening with sweat, toned body tanned and on display as he mowed the lawn and tended the plantings.

Garrett's hand fell to his crotch as he imagined watching shirtless, sweaty Drake doing yard work, then cooling off with the spray from the garden hose, getting soaking wet. That would make his jeans cling to his muscular legs and generous package. Garrett had snuck a glance or two at Drake's bulge while they had played at the arcade and liked what he had seen, only to have it confirmed by their session in the truck.

Maybe I'd bring him iced tea when he was working in the yard. He'd kiss me, and I'd protest a little about getting sweaty, even though I loved it.

He unzipped and slipped his hand inside his briefs, wrapping his fingers around his cock and starting a slow, steady rhythm slicked with pre-come as he imagined making out with Drake in the backyard, then the screened-in porch. He pictured going to his knees to suck Drake, pushing him against the wall, steadying him when his knees nearly buckled with the intensity of his climax.

In his imagination, Drake tackled him to the floor, pulling off Garrett's jeans and underwear and returning the favor, taking his time to suck his balls and then going back to a steady rhythm. When dream Drake took him into his throat and hollowed his cheeks, Garrett couldn't hold out any longer. He cried out Drake's name as he came, spilling over his fist, gasping for breath.

Afterward, he lay still for a few minutes, heart hammering, riding the high. He reached for his T-shirt and wiped off his hands and thighs. As good as the climax was, Garrett felt a surge of loneliness, wishing Drake had really been present.

We've got a date tomorrow night. Maybe I can get him to come home with me. I like him, and I really want to see where this can go.

Who knows? Maybe Drake will be the one I get to keep.

CHAPTER THREE

DRAKE

et down!
Drake saw a car swing out from the curb and head for him. Training and instinct vied with psychic abilities to shout a warning in his mind. He dropped to the pavement as three gunshots fired through the space where he had just been standing.

Before the car could back up or turn around, Drake sprang to his feet and jumped the hedge that edged the sidewalk. Weaving at full speed through backyards at an angle to the road, he dodged a friendly golden retriever and a highly skeptical boxer before emerging from beneath damp wash hanging on a clothesline in a back alley.

The dogs in the neighborhood set up a racket, barking at each other even if only two knew the real cause for commotion. Pretty soon raised voices shouted for quiet, bringing neighbors out onto their back steps.

Drake plastered himself against the side of a garage. He didn't think the shooter would continue pursuit with so many people outside for a late morning walk or try his luck chasing Drake down the long, narrow alley. The alley put the advantage with Drake and would give him a perfect shot to stop the driver, who couldn't turn around.

After several minutes, the dogs settled, and Drake figured the gunman had decided against the alley, even if he tried to guess Drake's route.

Still, Drake remained cautious, taking a circuitous route back to where he had parked his truck. He drove around in circles, going on and off exits until he felt sure no one was following him. He pulled into a car wash, scanned the truck for trackers, and used the high-pressure wand to remove one device that had been added just since he parked. He disabled it and bagged it as evidence.

Only then did he return to his hotel, more freaked out than he wanted to admit.

He went inside and scanned the room, relieved that nothing had been touched while he was gone. Drake dropped into a chair, put his now cold takeout meatball sub onto the desk, and let out a long breath.

"Holy shit."

The adrenaline of a close call dampened his appetite, and the zero appeal of a stone-cold sandwich meant he only choked down three-quarters of the sub before he gave up, saving the bag of chips and pickle and tossing the rest.

He dialed Faye's number, not surprised that she picked up on the first ring since she was the psychic who had tipped him off about the threat. "Are you okay?" she asked.

"Thanks for the heads-up. Saved my ass—or my head," Drake told the psychic. "No idea who the shooter was. They didn't hit me—but I was too busy staying alive to get their plates."

"That's all right. We'll figure it out. Glad you're not hurt," Faye told him.

Faye Miller had an impressive reputation as a psychic from a family of psychics—or as people in the mountains called it, conjure. Her great-great-great-grandparents had been part of the Mountain Cove spiritualist community back before the Civil War. When that experimental village failed, they moved north to Wheeling, where a small but supportive group of like-minded people quietly honed their paranormal talents and provided advice and healing to those who believed in clairvoyance and mediumship.

"Did you get any updates?" Drake asked.

"You, of all people, should know this doesn't work like email," Faye chided him fondly. "I don't control what I hear or when I hear it. But when the message concerns you, I let you know right away."

Drake sighed. "I know. And I appreciate it. I'm just a little weirded out."

"Understandable. Make any progress?"

Drake recapped what he had discovered thus far. "I still don't have a clear idea about who's working with whom and who might be the next big bad now that Willis Osborn is out of the picture."

"Patience. You're in the right place to learn more."

"Is that general encouragement or good vibes with a little something extra?" He wondered if her abilities had clued in.

"Hmm....there's something beside the case in Moundsville," Faye replied in the slightly sing-song tone her voice took on when she was relaying something revealed by her abilities. "You've met someone who interests you."

"I'm a federal agent. Almost everyone interests me," Drake evaded.

Faye clucked her tongue. "Not that way—I hope. A man. You like him. He likes you too."

"Good to know it's mutual. Do you get any vibes about

whether he's tangled up with the bad guys? I ran his plate and did a little database snooping. He seemed legit."

Faye let out an exaggerated sigh. "Misuse of government resources?"

"Not really. I'd hate to go to a movie with him and find out he's an assassin for the Mob."

Faye chuckled. "I don't pick up that sort of darkness around him. In fact, he gives off a lot of healing positive energy. Kindness. Loyalty. Use your head and keep your eyes open, but I'm not getting any warning signals."

"That's good," Drake confessed. "We had fun at the arcade. I'm seeing him again tonight." He usually kept his personal life out of the office, but he worked so closely with Clark and Faye that keeping a prospective partner a secret wasn't feasible. Especially given Faye's psychic abilities.

"That's a good thing," she encouraged. "You need more than work in your life."

Drake hesitated, then plunged on. "Am I putting him at risk, seeing him when I'm working a case?"

"Hmm." Faye was quiet for a moment. "Hard to see. By the time you've had a chance for anything serious to happen, you're likely to be back in Wheeling. And you're FBSI. There will always be another case, a different bad guy. A possible threat. It's like with cops and soldiers—it takes a certain kind of person to be their partner."

With a casual hook-up, Drake wouldn't have been worried that anyone watching might see an opportunity to hurt him or his date. But he had the feeling that Garrett could turn into something much more than a temporary distraction. Whether that was his own psychic intuition or just wishful thinking remained to be seen.

"Let me know what you hear on the Psychic Hotline," he joked.

"Hotline? Humph," Faye tossed back. "Don't worry—you will be the first to know."

Drake ended the call and let the conversation sink in. Having Faye vouch for Garrett underscored his gut feeling that his crush was okay. He felt relieved, glad that Garrett hadn't turned out to be either a bad risk or worse, a honey trap.

I'll just be extra careful, Drake told himself. *I don't think the witches will risk a large-scale massacre, so we're probably safe at the arcade. I've chosen a dangerous job. I can't spend my life hiding from risk.*

Speaking of which...I got distracted and didn't go through my list.

Drake checked the room for listening devices and cameras, then ran a separate EMP scan for anything ghostly. Relieved to find nothing, he made sure the doors and windows were locked, toed off his shoes, and poured himself a cup of coffee. Much as he wanted to add whiskey, he held off—for now.

Drake propped himself up in bed with his laptop and reached for his phone. "Hey, Clark," he said when his investigating partner picked up. "Turn up anything good from Charleston?"

"Maybe," Clark allowed, gruff as always. "Why do you sound out of breath?"

"Someone tried to shoot me. Drive-by. Could be random, but I strongly doubt it."

"You have that effect on people," Clark noted in a dry tone. "You okay?"

"Yeah. A little spooked, but that keeps me on my toes, I guess," Drake allowed. "Wish I knew whose camp the shooter was in. The syndicate? The drug cabal? Or the witchlings who want to take over for the big bad we got rid of here a few months ago."

"All of the above?" Clark suggested. "You need me to come over there?"

Drake thought for a moment. "No. That won't change anything. I'm guessing I've gotten close. I just wish I knew to what."

"Catch your breath, sit back, and I'll tell you what I found in Charleston," Clark said.

"I'm all ears."

"Willis Osborn, the warlock who got taken out by hunters a little while back, had a hell of an organization going across several states, including West Virginia," Clark said. "Not so hard to believe since he was based in Cleveland, and we're not far away. Plenty of shell companies and financial sleight of hand. He had wellness and vitamin companies to cover the paranormal pharmaceuticals and recreational drugs for shifter and vampire metabolisms. He also specialized in zombie drugs—ones that made it easier for witches and vampires—or creeps—to weaken a person's will and compel them.

"I'm sure there's more behind the scenes than what shows up officially," Clark continued, "but what I did find had links back to people with known paranormal abilities and the Supernatural Syndicate families."

"Surprise, surprise," Drake said in a dry tone.

"I know, right? He's also got a staffing company that I'm pretty sure is a cover for trafficking shifters and psychics."

"Real sleazeball."

"Yep. And that's in addition to the damage he was capable of doing directly as a pretty powerful witch," Clark agreed. "But if you recall, it turned out he was leeching juice from his old mentor's spirit, so not all of that magical power was his own. He was also pretty ruthless about squashing potential threats, so most witches with any real talent left the area. I suspect he strongly encouraged those relocations. There are still a few missing persons who might have been rival witches."

"Any luck finding out about the people at the top? I'm sure the syndicate families have their own witches."

Clark sighed. "You're probably right on the witches. As for the bigwigs, there are the acknowledged ones, and then there are always ones who hold power but stay out of the limelight. I combed through tax forms and financial documents looking for fingerprints and paper trails. I did come up with some new names I'm going to look into."

"Good stuff," Drake said.

"The rivalry is real. Of the known and suspected syndicate members, there's been a big uptick in murders and unexplained sudden deaths," Clark said. "It's a mob war, whether the normies want to acknowledge it or not."

"Any collateral damage yet? Someone's always in the wrong place at the wrong time." Drake felt a headache coming on.

"If they stick to targeted spells and curses, maybe not," Clark pointed out. "Most witches don't want to call attention to using magic, so they stay focused. Using an AK-47 approach to spellwork is going to get noticed. But a sudden heart attack here, an unexpected car accident there won't be as easy to spot."

"What next?" Drake rubbed his temples.

"Keep poking around, looking for weak links," Clark replied. "It's one of those 'we'll know it when we see it' things. Sooner or later, there's an opening."

"Don't forget to keep Faye in the loop," Drake reminded him.

"Don't worry—she's got spells and wards on me out the wazoo," Clark assured him.

"Didn't know you were quite so worried about your wazoo," Drake joked.

Clark gave an exaggerated, put-upon sigh. "You know what I meant."

"Yes, I did. Just let me know if you get a break in the case. I'll keep poking around here—"

"Being a target?"

"That, too," Drake said. "Be careful—we don't know who's shooting at us yet."

"Yeah. Don't worry about me. Just watch your back."

Drake ended the call and got up to pour another cup of coffee. Clark and Faye were his closest contacts and had been since his move to Wheeling. A former cop, Clark knew the ins and outs of working with the police and who to avoid. He did excellent research, was good with a gun, and didn't give a damn that Drake was gay.

Neither did Faye, whose abilities had saved their asses more than once and whose wardings, spells, and protections gave Drake a much higher likelihood of living long enough to see retirement.

Drake spent the next few hours doing email, including a recap for his boss, and following up on the alerts he had set to gather information on the players he was tracking in Moundsville. He knew that the big break in cases often came from small details that showed up unexpectedly.

It's like looking for a needle in a haystack if you don't even know what a needle looks like or which haystack it's in.

Still, it was the excitement of the chase that had attracted Drake to law enforcement in the first place. Also the chance to use his psychic abilities appealed to him. He knew he could have gone into finance, investment, or other careers where flashes of foresight or intuition could be more lucrative, and on bad days, he questioned his choices.

But on better days, Drake liked knowing that he was helping people, stopping criminals, and making a corner of the world a little better.

The alarm on his phone went off, warning him that it was time to get ready for his date with Garrett.

Last time was a pick-up. This is a real date. Does the difference matter?

Drake had spent the years since joining the bureau avoiding personal entanglements. In hindsight, more time had slipped away than he intended. He had never wanted to be single forever, but between busy investigations and temporary assignments, the years passed quickly.

Too quickly. He knew plenty of senior agents who had never married or had a track record of multiple divorces. The life definitely required a certain kind of partner. Drake had always wondered if those agents who remained single never wanted a committed relationship, or if they just hadn't found the right person—or couldn't change themselves enough to accommodate someone else.

Drake swore he would never let that happen to him. Yet here he was, in his mid-thirties and still unattached. Other than one-night stands and some occasional hurried encounters at bars, his love life until now had been DOA.

That wasn't what he wanted long-term. While Drake couldn't see himself in the traditional roles his parents had followed, he could imagine that with the right partner, they could chart their own course, figure out what worked for them.

Most of the time, Drake had been able to squelch his desire for a forever partner in pursuit of the case. That he couldn't now, that thinking about Garrett after just two days had become a constant, suggested that his intuition was trying hard to give him a message.

Garrett's probably a little younger. What if he's not ready to get serious?

Drake felt surprised at how sharp the disappointment felt at that thought.

So far, he seems to be enthusiastically on board.

I'm a big, bad FBSI agent. I hunt monsters. I kill vampires. Going on a date shouldn't make me wobbly.

Drake tried to clear his mind as he showered. He took extra time to do more manscaping than he usually bothered with if there was no one to notice. Unsure how their date might end, but hopeful of going further than the last time, he cleaned thoroughly inside and out.

Despite the preconceptions about alpha male government agents, Drake liked to switch with the right partner under the right circumstances. For quickies and one-night stands that went beyond jerking off or blow jobs, he topped. In the very few relationships he'd had that lasted more than a couple of weeks, where he had built up a level of trust, he had been willing to bottom and enjoyed it with a partner who knew what to do to make sure both of them had a good fuck.

He got out of the shower and dried off, then stared in the mirror trying to decide whether to go clean-shaven or leave the stubble.

"Stubble," he said to himself, surprised at how nervous he felt.

God, this is worse than senior prom. I need to get a grip.

He dried his hair, taking more time with it than usual. Drake stood in front of the mirror, debating the choice of shirt and which jeans made his ass look particularly good.

"Condoms." He returned to the bathroom and rummaged in his travel kit. Drake tucked three into his wallet, feeling optimistic.

He questioned adding a spritz of cologne and wondered if it had been so long that the small vial in his kit had dried up. It hadn't, and Drake threw caution to the wind and chanced a short spray.

"Aw, shit. The truck."

Drake checked the time and assured himself he had

enough leeway to do a quick clean-up of the inside of his Silverado, although tonight he hoped they found a better place to get acquainted than the backseat.

He wasn't ready to bring Garrett back to his hotel room just yet. Drake wasn't really concerned about Garrett trying to hack into his computer or riffle through his case files. His intuition and Faye's agreement muted those fears.

But if someone was watching him because of the case, he didn't want to attract undue attention or draw the stalker's eye to Garrett. Much better to get another room—or go back to Garrett's place if that was on offer.

A beep from his phone told him it was time to go. Drake stole another glance in the mirror, told himself not to be a teenager about things, and locked up.

Garrett was waiting for him in the lobby of the arcade, playing a machine with a grabber-hand and failing to snatch one of the small stuffed animals in the bin.

"No luck?" Drake came up behind Garrett.

"Not yet, but I might get lucky later." Garrett grinned and winked.

"I was thinking that after we eat, bowl a little, and play a game or two of billiards, we could go check out that new carnival that just pitched its tents," Drake said. "I checked the hours—we're starting early enough here that it should still be open for us to go over later."

"Carnival? Sounds good. Is it haunted? I just watched a series on streaming like that. Spooky—and really good," Garrett said. Drake couldn't help grinning at his date's enthusiasm.

They ate a dinner of Buffalo wings and fried pickles at the bar, then started with billiards. Drake hadn't played since college, and even then, he had been shaky on the rules. Garrett didn't seem any better versed, so they just tried to have a good time.

"I'd be happy to sink your balls in my pocket," Garrett teased in a quiet voice as he passed behind Drake on the way to make a shot.

In response, Drake caught his eye and ran his cue in and out of a circle made by the thumb and forefinger of his left hand.

"Sounds like the kind of game where everyone goes home happy." Garrett took the next shot.

They didn't bother keeping score since neither of them was sure of the rules and played until all the balls had been sunk. They were both laughing and teasing by the time they returned the cues to the game desk.

"Let's play with the big balls next," Drake teased. "It's easier to get a grip."

"It's just good technique to use all three fingers," Garrett replied, meeting Drake's gaze without flinching. Drake felt blood rise in his cheeks—and in his cock. "Just be careful—no one wants blue balls."

At least in bowling, they were both somewhat familiar with the rules and how to keep score.

"I haven't bowled since high school." Drake sent his bright red ball careening down the alley, only to end up in the gutter.

"Same here." Garrett's green ball managed to stay on the alley but only knocked down one pin.

Since it was a weeknight, the arcade wasn't nearly as busy as on a weekend, so they weren't rushed to finish their game. Garrett came back from the bar with a beer for each of them as Drake filled out the scorecard.

"This is fun, but I draw the line at those matching league shirts," Garrett warned.

"How about the trendy shoes?" Drake stuck out one bowling-shoe-clad foot and wiggled it.

"It might pass for self-aware kitsch, but I wouldn't bet on

it." Garrett tilted his head back and took a long drink of his beer.

Drake couldn't help watching his throat work and getting all kinds of ideas unsuitable for being in public.

If they relied on Drake's highly dubious scoring of the billiards game and their bowling match, they each won one game. Neither of them cared enough to verify the numbers and left it at that as they headed back to their vehicles.

"We could drop off my Suburban at my place and go to the carnival in yours—if you're okay with coming back to my apartment afterward," Garrett offered.

Drake grinned. "I think that makes a lot of sense. I'll follow you. Lead the way."

As he drove, he thought of how much fun they had at the arcade and how effortless it felt just being together. They hit it off, and Drake felt accepted. That stopped the constant questioning he often felt on other dates over whether he was being too much of a nerd or somehow not being suave enough.

Garrett's place was a modernized duplex with an inviting front porch. He parallel-parked in front on the first try, locked the SUV, and got into Drake's truck.

"Nice parking," Drake said. "I'd have taken half a dozen back-and-forths."

"I get lots of practice," Garrett replied, but he still grinned and blushed a little. "So...tell me about this carnival."

"I saw an ad somewhere for the Carnival of Mysteries, and I thought it sounded spooky and fun," Drake replied. "We got an early start on dinner and the arcade, so there should be plenty of time to explore."

"I haven't been to a fair or an amusement park in too long. When I was a kid, my family would do one or both things at least once each summer. Then once I was in high school, I went with friends. But there wasn't anywhere close when I was in college, and I worked summers and...I just quit going."

"Me, too. There was a county fair that was always a treat to explore when I was a kid," Drake recalled. "Cotton candy, corn dogs, fudge—I ate my way around the midway and then wondered why I got queasy on the rides!"

He didn't mention his teenage crush on one of the ride attendants who was the same age and how they would sneak behind the tents for hurried hand jobs before the fair finally moved on.

"Do you know anyone who's gone to the Carnival of Mysteries?"

Now that Drake thought about it, he didn't. But he had seen posters and ads, although at the moment, he couldn't remember where. *Not online, I don't think. Must have been a billboard or one of those signs on the side of a bus. Maybe a poster in a restaurant.*

"No, but it's an excuse to walk outside on a nice night," Drake reached over to take Garrett's hand as he drove. "We'll make it around the circle, and if it's boring, we leave early."

The carnival had set up its tents on a large, open field on the outskirts of town. Some of the tents were new and brightly colored, while others looked much older.

A white cloth banner suspended over the entrance proclaimed, "Welcome, Traveler." They found a parking spot and headed toward the gate. Drake didn't feel comfortable taking Garrett's hand in so public a place, but he let his brush against the back of Garrett's knuckles and briefly linked their pinky fingers before letting go. Garrett didn't pull away.

"I'm surprised there's no fence," Drake remarked. He spotted a ticket booth and headed that way. Carousel music carried on the breeze, along with the smell of fresh popcorn.

"Wow—it's old school," Garrett said as they got their

tickets and approached the gate, with a touch of awe in his tone.

Drake hesitated once they got about six feet from the gate as a strong wave of supernatural energy washed over him.

"You okay?" Garrett asked, likely noticing the pause.

"Yeah. Just thought of something I need to remember to do when I get home." Drake sidestepped the question. He intended to check his sources about the carnival and talk to others who might know more because all of his psychic senses told him the event wasn't mundane.

"It looks amazing. I hope the junk food is good—that's half the fun." Garrett's enthusiasm was clear in his voice.

Drake swept his senses as broadly as he could over the fair. He picked up on active magic and illusion, as well as an undercurrent of paranormal energy, but nothing that struck him as dangerous or malicious.

He tried not to remember all the made-for-TV movies he had seen as a kid about haunted fairgrounds, killer clowns, and faerie festivals that whisked unwary visitors away to another realm.

Drake blinked, and the nearly overwhelming sensations dropped to be barely noticeable.

Did its magic sense mine and adjust? That's...creepy.

Garrett tugged at his sleeve to hurry, and Drake couldn't come up with a plausible reason to turn back now. He was glad he always had silver, salt, iron, and holy water in his pockets. Even in small quantities, they could make all the difference if he got in a bad situation with ghosts or malicious spirits.

Not the conversation I want to have with Garrett right now—or at least, just yet. There will be plenty of time to tell him if we stay an item.

Drake felt a frisson of magic when they walked beneath the banner as if they had crossed a warded threshold. A glance at Garrett told him his companion didn't notice anything strange.

"Welcome to the Carnival of Mysteries!" the man in the ticket booth said, stepping out to greet them. He wore an old-fashioned red-and-white striped barker's shirt with a bowtie and a straw hat. "Get your tickets here."

Drake paid for the tickets, and Garrett insisted he would pick up the tab on their next date.

The man in the ticket booth made Drake's intuition tingle, not with perceived threat but with the awareness of something outside the range of normal.

Is he a witch? A shifter? Hopefully not a vampire—I think I saw that movie.

"The rides, games, and food are in the middle, along with the big top. Tents for special exhibits are around the perimeter," the man told them as he handed Drake the tickets. For an instant, their hands touched, and Drake nearly yelped with the odd glimmer of power that passed between them in a fraction of a second.

"I can tell you have very good sight," the man said with a smile and a look in his eyes that suggested a second meaning to his comment. "There will be a lot for you to see here—and unlike so many pretenders, everything here is *real*."

Drake stifled a gasp. The ticket seller had some sort of magic, and he had recognized that Drake did too. *Was that a welcome or a warning?* Drake wondered.

"Don't let our strange and wonderful exhibits make you nervous," the man continued, as if he could guess—or read— Drake's thoughts. "Within these gates, you and your companion are safe." He held Drake's gaze for an instant too long, and Drake wondered if he should take some sort of special meaning from the man's words.

Garrett plucked at Drake's sleeve. "Come on! This looks really cool."

Inside the grounds, the energy fell to a dull hum in the back of Drake's mind, nonthreatening but still present. He wondered if it was a protective warding or if it somehow enhanced the attractions in the carnival.

Garrett half-led, half-dragged Drake excitedly toward the midway. Classic carnival games lined the avenue on both sides, full of bright-colored signs and waving flags. Strings of overhead lights crisscrossed the thoroughfare, and the glow of neon from the rides lit the night. Music from a calliope carried on the air, along with the scent of fresh popcorn and the tang of hot dogs.

"Let's play." Garrett stopped in front of a balloon pop stall. He plopped down the money to pay for both of them. "My treat."

"Pop a green balloon, get a ride ticket," the barker told them. "Blue is a food credit or something from the prize tent. Pink is a free tarot or palm reading with Madame Persephone." Drake noted that there were a lot of green balloons lower on the backboard, with fewer and higher blue targets and a single line of pink at the very top.

"Fortune favors the bold," he told them with a mysterious smile. Drake felt *seen* and wondered if everyone here had some sort of psychic ability.

He and Garrett took their darts and eyed the targets. Garrett's first throw missed, but then he hit a green and a blue. Drake hit blue, and then to his surprise, popped a pink balloon he hadn't even aimed for.

"Congratulations." The barker handed out their prizes but held onto the pink prize for an instant longer before passing it on.

"You'll find Madame Persephone in her purple tent along the outer circle. A wise man can distinguish which things here are diversions and which are real." The man's words sounded more like a warning than mere instructions, and Drake tried not to shiver.

The next game, a shooting gallery, used air guns styled to look like rifles to fire at rows of moving targets. Instead of the usual bears, clowns, and bullseyes, these were vampires, werewolves, and ghosts.

"They definitely lean into the whole mysteries thing." Garrett took aim at a row of slavering werewolves.

For the record, they don't really look like that, Drake thought.

"Good shot!"

Drake had hit several targets. Garrett's aim wasn't true, but he didn't seem to care, and Drake walked away with more tickets.

At the ring toss, they both scored, even though the posts to catch the rings were the prongs of antlers on nightmarish deer creatures. Their luck held at the bottle knock-down—where all the bottles were labeled with skulls and crossbones. In the next booth, vultures on nests floated past instead of yellow ducks with the prize marked on the bottom.

"We won things!" Garrett exulted. "This is the best fair ever. I never win anything. What do you want to use the tickets on?"

"You can cash them in at any stall or ride on the midway." The barker bore an uncanny resemblance to several of the other attendants, making Drake wonder if the carnival was a family affair. "Or trade for a prize in the tent at the end of the row."

"I want a souvenir to remember tonight." Garrett's eyes shone with excitement. His enthusiasm was contagious, and while Drake didn't let down his guard completely, he still hadn't picked up on any indication that they were in danger. If anything, inside the warded territory of the carnival, he felt safe and recharged.

Garrett led them into the rewards tent, where an attendant dressed in black oversaw bins with prizes of all shapes and sizes. He carefully counted out the tickets, giving half to each. "Pick something to remember me by," he told Drake with such excitement that Drake couldn't help getting carried along.

Although the prizes were the types normally found in arcades—stickers, rub-on tattoos, polished gemstones, inexpensive pendants—Drake noticed that the patterns were far from random. He recognized the sigils and runes as old, protective magic from a variety of traditions, and the shiny stones as being known to ward off evil and have healing properties. They both picked polished worry stones made of garnet and onyx, easy to keep in a pocket.

"Don't miss the aerialist show," the attendant told them. "It's starting now in the big top. You can make it if you hurry."

They thanked him and returned to the midway, walking close enough that their shoulders bumped.

"Good evening, and welcome to the Carnival of Mysteries." The man made eye contact with them as if Drake and Garrett were the only guests on the midway. He was around Drake's height, slender, with dark olive skin, black hair, and black eyes. His puffy-sleeved white laced-up shirt contrasted with black breeches, boots, and velvet vest.

"I am the carnival master, Errante Ame. Here among my people, you are under my protection as you take in wonders and oddities you will find nowhere else. Explore our illusions. Challenge your certainty. Seek your fortune. You can do all that—and more—within our festival."

Drake felt a sudden warmth as if Errante had read his soul. He was surprised that he felt safe instead of exposed, as if here, nothing could harm them.

Before he could react, the man walked off, leaving Drake pondering the odd encounter.

"Come on," Garrett urged. "If it's boring, we can sneak out. I want to get the food and rides we've won before things close."

The big top stood taller than everything else in the heart of the fairgrounds, making it easy to find. They slipped into the back of the big tent, getting seats at the end of a row in case they didn't stay. For a weeknight, there was a pretty good crowd, in addition to the people Drake had seen milling about outside.

Strings of bulbs stretched between the support posts, casting the interior in a warm glow and highlighting the white and red stripes of the canvas. Red climbing scarves dangled from steel bars secured near the peak, going far higher than Drake would be comfortable free-climbing.

Music started, traditional circus tunes, and half a dozen aerialists clad in iridescent bodysuits emerged from a side entrance and paraded around the center area to give everyone a good look. Tall, dark-haired, and green-eyed, they were clearly related to one another.

"Welcome, travelers, to the Carnival of Mysteries!" the ringmaster said in a booming baritone voice. He was a handsome man in his thirties with tanned skin, dark hair, and brown eyes. He wore a classic ringmaster's outfit, with a red jacket, white shirt, top hat, breeches, and boots.

"Prepare to be amazed and astounded! To be awed and to question the bounds of reality as you comprehend it." He was an arresting figure with a consummate stage presence. Drake wondered if the man's voice held a light compulsion, overlaying his natural ability to work a crowd.

"I am Rafe, the Ringmaster, your guide to the shows under the big top and along our midway." Rafe turned slowly as he spoke. His gaze swept the bleachers, and Drake felt the man's eyes rest on him, pausing a little longer as if trying to make sense of what he saw. Once again, Drake felt uncomfortably visible but not threatened, more like he presented a puzzle for the ringmaster to resolve.

"Travel the world or the galaxy, visit diverse realms and realities; you will not find a show to equal what you will see here at the Carnival of Mysteries!"

The trappings of the tent and the music raised spooky Halloween vibes. Even the costumes of the aerialists were designed to be different and a little unsettling. Then the performers walked out into the ring to thunderous applause.

Despite his reservations, Drake found himself entranced as he watched the gymnasts perform high above the ground on the climbing silks. They moved fearlessly and with grace, then did daring switches between silks and wrapped themselves up only to rapidly drop as they unrolled, making Drake and Garrett catch their breath.

The audience roared and clapped. Drake and Garrett showed their enthusiasm along with everyone else, although in between, when their hands were out of sight on the bench, Drake linked their pinky fingers and felt heartened when Garrett didn't pull away.

When the show ended, Drake and Garrett headed to the food booths to cash in their tickets on cotton candy, fried cheese curd, and a soft pretzel with mustard.

They made a slow circuit of the midway, stopping to watch a show by Darius the Wonder Dog. After seeing the performance, in which Darius's handler seemed more for show than controlling the act, Drake came away seriously wondering if Darius might be something more arcane than a normal dog.

The strong man show again made Drake question whether the entire carnival was made up of people with supernatural abilities. That feeling grew stronger when they watched the stage show performed by The Amazing

Mephistopheles, which Drake felt certain utilized real magic rather than sleight of hand.

Despite the paranormal elements, Drake felt safe, and while he had seen plenty of movies about sinister traveling shows, the carnival felt more like a haven.

Drake and Garrett checked out the rides, opting for a turn on the massive, ornate carousel complete with unicorns, dragons, and other fantastic beasts, all of which looked hand-carved and were beautifully painted. They decided to skip the swings and slide. The fun house was old school, with mirrored rooms, moving floors, and jump scares. Drake didn't mind at all when Garrett crowded closer, grabbing his arm.

They stopped outside the haunted house, and while it looked like a gaudy ride-through attraction, Drake felt uneasy, sensing both a touch of magic and a chill of spirits. By unspoken agreement, they skipped it and shared a funnel cake instead.

"Let's go talk to the tarot reader." Garrett nudged Drake toward the tents in the outer ring. "It'll be fun."

"Do you believe in that kind of thing?" Drake found himself holding his breath, knowing that Garrett's answer would suggest his reaction if Drake shared about his abilities.

"Yes—and no," Garrett replied as they meandered. "I think that it's very possible that real psychic abilities exist—and mediumship, too. Is it as common as every street fair, and do they work for 1-900 phone hotlines? Probably not."

Drake could live with a sensible answer that left room to be convinced. He was relieved that Garrett wasn't too much of a believer because there were plenty of frauds. To Drake's mind, the frauds weren't as dangerous as the psychics who used their abilities to manipulate or steal.

He wondered what they would find when they reached Madame Persephone's tent. Would she be a good actress, picking up on verbal and non-verbal cues to give answers that sounded good enough to believe? Did she have a bit of talent, enough to fish answers and insights from the ether?

More importantly—would she recognize Drake for what he was?

"Here we are." Garrett stopped in front of the fortune-teller's tent. Drake watched him for any sign that Garrett picked up on any strange vibes, but he barely hesitated before leading the way inside.

"Welcome," a man greeted them as they stepped into a small area set off from the main tent with a curtain. "Please, have a seat. Madame will be with you shortly."

"You never said whether or not you believed." Garrett turned to Drake as they took their seats. "Do you?"

"I've had experiences that make me think it's real." Drake worded his response carefully. "And I have some friends who I absolutely believe have gifts."

He wasn't quite ready to admit his own dreams and visions but figured agreeing on qualified belief in the supernatural was a good start.

They hadn't waited long before the man returned.

"Madame will see you now." He held the curtain aside and ushered them into the inner chamber.

A woman sat at a table draped in a purple cloth with gold embroidered tarot symbols around the hem. He had difficulty figuring her age and guessed mid-thirties, although for a second in the soft, shifting candlelight, she looked much older. She wore colorful flowing robes that fit with the mystical opulence of the tent. Rings glittered on her fingers —silver, onyx, garnet, opal—all valued for protection and enhancing magic. The air smelled of vervain, mint, and rosemary, more protective plants.

The tent was fairly dark despite the candles. Around the sides, gauzy swags of fabric were tinted in colors that appeared to shift and swirl. Drake thought he could pick out symbols amid the colors associated with several traditions of old magic. The tent's soothing atmosphere made him feel like he was in a light trance. He put more than the requested fee in the ornate box on a small table right inside the door.

Madame Persephone raised her head and looked right at Drake. "Welcome, I expected you sooner."

Drake might have written off the comment as a script designed to increase trust, but Madame met his gaze, and he felt her power touch him. *She's the real deal—and she's older and more powerful than she lets on. Way more than a carnival act.*

"I'd like you to tell my fortune," Garrett blurted. "Cards, palm, whatever you prefer."

The table in front of the seer held a crystal ball and a deck of cards. On a smaller table to her right lay a collection of crystals, a drop spindle, and a pile of wool roving. Drake recognized the last two as an ancient form of divination and wondered again about the power and age of their host.

"Give me your hand."

Garrett reached out, and Madame took his right hand. Drake fought the urge to grab Garrett and run, worried what she might learn.

Madame closed her eyes, and a look of concentration came over her face. "You have left your family, but you are not alone. You're a healer, and your intuition is stronger than you realize. You advocate for those who cannot speak. But you have also known darkness. A shadow lingers, persistent. It is not done with you. And yet…"

She opened her eyes and took Drake's hand before he could pull away. "There is new light that shines very brightly," she added with a knowing look directed at Drake. "A protector. And a bond, untested but unusually strong. Uncommon. Nothing that brought you together happened by chance."

Drake felt poleaxed, and a glance at Garrett confirmed that his date had gotten more than he expected.

"There are dangers ahead you cannot avoid. Do not give up hope. A path exists to lead you to what you desire, but finding the way and remaining on it will test you."

Madame let go of their hands, and Drake felt the absence of her energy like a physical loss. She looked directly at Drake.

"Your quarry is strong and clever. Do not underestimate him."

Drake found himself holding his breath. The air seemed to crackle around them with psychic energy and magic, enough to raise the hair on his arms. He didn't fear Madame, but he respected her power and wondered how much she could be trusted.

"My Sight is not something to worry you. Stay close to one another," she said as if she could read his mind.

Maybe she can.

"A storm is coming, and such things are best ridden out together," she added. "Remain watchful."

"Um, thank you," Garrett stuttered, grabbed Drake by the wrist, and headed for the tent door.

"You are safe here," Madame called after them. "Remember that when you need sanctuary."

Garrett didn't stop practically dragging Drake until they were several tents away. "Oh. My. God," he said, breathless. "What was that?"

"I suspect *that* was an encounter with someone who is actually a fairly powerful clairvoyant." Drake was a little rattled himself by the reading. "For what it's worth, I didn't sense any danger. In fact, I believe her about this being a safe place. I think there are more than a few people with the carnival who have different kinds of psychic abilities. But I don't think they're a threat."

Garrett seemed to consider his words for a moment. "Then why am I freaked out?" He seemed more curious than concerned.

"If it's your first time meeting someone with that sort of ability, it can be unnerving," Drake answered. "I think we've got some sort of hindbrain wiring to sense that energy and be wary of it."

The path around them wasn't crowded, so they could talk without being overheard. "Why didn't it freak you out?" Garrett looked at Drake more closely for a few seconds. "You have some ability too."

Drake had no intention of lying. If what he could do was going to be a deal breaker, better to find it out now, before he became even more emotionally invested. "Yes. Different from Madame, but real and fairly strong."

Garrett took a deep breath. "Okay."

"Is it? I can explain some things, not others, and I can try to help you understand, but is this going to be a problem... for us?" Drake's heart sank. He really liked Garrett and had found himself daydreaming more and more that they could build a real relationship.

"No. Of course not," Garrett answered quickly enough that Drake felt reassured. "It just surprised me. Although I think we should talk. I have questions." He ran a hand through his hair. "That doesn't sound nearly like the sexy evening I was hoping for."

"You never know. Depends."

"On what?"

"How the conversation goes. Still want me to come back to your place?" Drake felt nervousness curdle in his stomach, hoping the answer hadn't changed.

"Yes. Sure. I don't think it's really a car chat." He glanced around the carnival. They hadn't covered most of it. "Maybe we can come back."

"That could be fun. I'm curious to see what else is here," Drake agreed, as much out of a professional capacity as because it would be interesting to see with Garrett. He intended to check into official resources to see what anyone knew about the carnival. Drake suspected the faire had a knack for flying under the radar.

The ride back to Garrett's place was quiet. Drake tried to squelch his nervousness and failed.

I knew the conversation would have to happen sooner or later. I just wasn't prepared for it tonight.

CHAPTER FOUR

DRAKE

*a*n excited black lab mix met them at the door, wiggling and wagging.

"Drake, meet Bailey. Bailey, this is Drake." Garrett glanced to Drake. "I hope you like dogs. He comes with the deal."

"Absolutely." Drake dropped to one knee and let Bailey sniff his hand before reaching to scratch his ears. "Bailey looks like a very good boy."

"He is." Garrett fondly patted the dog on the head. "We've been through a lot together. Can I get you a drink?"

The vibe between them felt oddly awkward. "Beer, please." Drake wanted to be able to drive back to his hotel if things didn't go well. And if they didn't, he had bourbon in his room to dull the ache.

They sat down at the kitchen table, and Garrett picked at the label of his beer. "So…I guess we never talked about what we do for a living. I'm a veterinarian. I own a practice that works with small animals—pets that aren't exotic. That's pretty much been my life for the last five years.

"But as proud of the practice as I am, I want more in my life. Which is how I ended up at the bar, hoping to meet someone." His eyes widened. "Not that I'm in a rush. I know it's early for us. But I'll just put my cards on the table and say that, down the line, I want a real relationship."

Drake admired Garrett's honesty and appreciated his willingness to say what he wanted up front. He knew better than to say so, but he had learned about Garrett's profession and quite a bit about his past when he ran a background check. That sort of thing weirded out civilians, but Drake needed to make sure Garrett was who he claimed to be.

"That's actually how I got Bailey," Garrett continued. "I was adrift after my last relationship broke up. Bailey's family developed severe allergies and couldn't keep the dog. Bailey was a patient of mine, and the family asked if I could help find him a new home." He petted Bailey's back, and the dog stretched. "Bailey comes to the office with me most days," Garrett said. "He's sort of our mascot. He likes that better than being home alone."

"Understandable."

The conversation lagged, and Drake knew it was his turn to say something. Bailey got a drink of water from his bowl and curled up beneath the table.

"I work for a branch of law enforcement that deals with the paranormal." Drake chose his words carefully. "I can't say more, sorry. I'm normally based in Wheeling, but I'm here looking into some things. I went to the bar just wanting a drink and couldn't take my eyes off you."

He paused. "I don't seem to do anything in my life casually. I don't like one-night stands. I'd prefer an actual relationship, but for a long time, I put everything into the job. It has times that it's all-consuming, but I'm ready to not make it my only focus. I want more."

Drake cleared his throat. "That doesn't mean I'm going to try to pressure you into something or make this into something it isn't. But if you're open to the possibility—"

Garrett smiled and reached for his hand across the table. "I'm very open to that. And I'm fine with taking it one day at a time. Do you know how long you'll be in Moundsville?"

Drake shook his head. "No. Until the case is done. But Wheeling isn't far away."

"My office and the hospital are established here. They aren't something I can easily move—and I wouldn't want to. I love my patients, and I have a great staff," Garrett said, and Drake saw hesitation in his eyes as if that might be a deal breaker.

"I don't think that's a problem. Sometimes, like now, I have to travel for work. But my home base is Wheeling and if things work out, we could find a place that splits the drive for both of us."

On one hand, Drake felt like things were moving too fast and that they were getting ahead of themselves on what was barely the second date.

Then again, we're grown-ups with responsibilities, and free time is scarce. I think we're both at the point where we don't want to invest in a relationship that can't work out. Best to have the conversation up front so there's less of a mess to clean up.

Garrett was quiet, and Drake figured maybe he had said too much. "Uh, say something?"

Garrett pulled out of his thoughts with a self-conscious expression. "Sorry—my brain went off on a tangent. You're right. Wheeling isn't far depending on what end of town. So that could work. Now that we've got that figured out, you know I'm a vet, and I know you're not a spy; we can just take things as they come."

Drake winced at the word spy. Garrett picked up on it.

"*Are* you a spy?"

Drake shook his head. "Government agent specializing in paranormal problems. Not a spy. I swear."

Throughout their conversation, his internal radar didn't

ping on anything that made him think Garrett was being untruthful. He tried to return the favor to the best of his ability. If they really became serious, at some point he would say more about his job. But especially now, he didn't want to accidentally make Garrett a target.

"Are we good?" Garrett asked after a long pause as they finished their drinks.

"I am if you are," Drake replied.

Garrett let out his breath in a whoosh. "Okay, then. I'm glad. Because I enjoy being with you and I had fun tonight. And if the mood isn't totally ruined, I'd like to take off your clothes and make you feel good."

"I'm in favor of that."

Garrett's eyes widened as if he had said too much. "I mean, we can take things at whatever speed you want…no pressure…God, why am I so bad at this?"

Drake chuckled. "No worse than I am. I agree. There's no rush to hit milestones, although I'd be lying if I said that when the time's right, I'd like to fuck your brains out."

"See, we're already on the same wavelength. I'd like that at some point too." Garrett had an adorable spot of color blooming on his cheeks.

"Now that the heavy lifting is out of the way, will you stay the night?" Garrett asked.

"I'd love to." Drake couldn't hold back the smile.

Garrett fetched two more drinks and set them on the table. "Before we move on to other diversions…what did you make of what Madame said?"

Drake thought back over the seer's comments and what they had already discussed. "She seemed to sense a connection between us—which is a positive—and she wasn't warning us away from it. In fact, she seemed to see it as a protection."

"I'm just a veterinarian. You're a secret agent. I'm not much use for protecting anyone, sorry to say."

"She said you had a shadow," Drake recalled. "Do you know what she meant?"

Garrett shook his head. "No. I don't have any crazy exes, nobody out to get me—that I know about, anyhow."

"I'll do my very best to keep you safe," Drake promised. "And since we're 'fessing up—my work can be dangerous. Bad people shoot at me. I shoot back. Plenty of agents have partners and even families—but many of them don't because the life can be a lot to deal with."

Garrett nodded. "I can see that. Then again, a vet I know got shot by a patient because he couldn't save the man's dog. We live in a crazy world. I'm ready to take a few risks…for the right guy." He smiled, clearly flirting to lighten the moment.

"And do you think I could be the right guy?" Drake usually doubted his bantering skills, but with Garrett, it didn't feel forced. He opened up his gift to read Garrett's aura, something he had resisted until now beyond a quick peek to make sure there wasn't anything dark. Garrett's aura pulsed a warm orange-red, resonating with happiness, relaxation…and attraction.

"I sure would like to find out."

Garrett fed Bailey and took him out for a brief run in the backyard. When they came back inside, Bailey curled up on a dog bed next to the television and fell asleep.

They took their drinks into the living room and Garrett flipped through the menu until he found a sci-fi movie they had both seen multiple times, a comfortable background filler.

They snuggled together, sipping their drinks as their hands roamed. Drake nearly choked on his drink when

Garrett cupped his package with a light squeeze. He set his glass aside.

"What did you have in mind?" His voice was low and gravelly, which had nothing to do with the alcohol.

"I want to suck you. Is that okay?"

"Better than okay. And I want to return the favor," Drake replied with a hungry grin.

Garrett raised his head and looked toward where Bailey slept on his dog cushion. "Let's go in the bedroom. I…haven't brought anyone else home, and I don't want Bailey to misunderstand."

Drake's heartbeat sped up, and he fought a grin at the thought. *I like him. Enough that I don't want to share him. I might just want to keep him forever.*

"We don't want him getting jealous," Drake replied in a serious tone. Garrett gave him a look, likely trying to decide if he was making fun.

Drake raised his hands in surrender. "Seriously. A friend of mine got bitten that way—someone's dog thought all that moving around and making noise was an attack. I can't imagine how that went over in the emergency room."

Garrett rolled his eyes. "I'm hoping that the ER didn't do more than make a note of the circumstances. I can't guarantee something like that didn't get discussed in the break room, but definitely *not* in front of the patient."

Bailey lifted his head when they turned off the television and left the couch, but then he rolled over and kicked his feet into the air, apparently deciding they weren't interesting enough to follow.

Just for good measure, Garrett closed the bedroom door and latched it. "I, um, cleaned up and made the bed. Just in case." He blushed adorably.

Drake pulled Garrett into his arms and kissed him. "Were you hoping to get lucky?" he teased.

"Definitely hoping." Garrett kissed him back, making the response long and lingering.

"We can take things at whatever speed you're comfortable with. There's no timeline." Drake deepened the kiss.

Although he was eager to get to know Garrett and learn what made him happy in bed, Drake was fine with taking things slowly, especially if Garrett hadn't been very active in the years he was building his vet practice.

Drake pushed Garrett against the wall and sank to his knees. He kept eye contact as he opened Garrett's belt and undid his zipper, taking his time. He pushed Garrett's jeans and briefs down to his ankles, and Garrett stepped out of one side, giving him room to spread his legs a bit.

Garrett might not have taken it for granted that they would spend the night together, but he was neatly trimmed and smelled more of soap than sweat. Drake appreciated the effort, but he missed the sharp tang that was uniquely Garrett.

"Fuck, you're beautiful." He wrapped his hand around the base of Garrett's erection, appreciating the length and girth, the slight curve, and the heft. Before Garrett could answer, Drake took him down to the root, making a pleased sound as Garrett moaned.

"Yeah. Just like that. Oh, fuck. So good."

Drake tried to ignore his own hard-on and shifted his hips for relief. He sucked and licked, hollowing his cheeks and bobbing up and down until Garrett gave up on words and groaned his pleasure.

"I'm close," Garrett warned.

Drake kept going, tracing the veins with his tongue, teasing at the sensitive spot beneath the head, and fondling Garrett's balls. Garrett tangled one hand in Drake's hair and gasped as his orgasm swept over him, fucking Drake's mouth as come shot down his throat.

Drake swallowed it all, moving his hands to grip Garrett's ass cheeks, working him through the aftershocks despite the ache in his own cock.

Garrett loosened his grip, stroking his fingers through Drake's hair instead of grabbing it tight. Drake let the softened cock slip from his mouth and nuzzled against Garrett's groin, getting a yelp of surprise when he licked too-sensitive balls.

"That was…yeah. Really good," Garrett said breathlessly. "Let me return the favor."

He guided Drake to sit on the end of the bed, helping him shimmy out of his pants and boxer briefs.

Drake obligingly spread his legs. "Like what you see?"

"Oh, hell yes." He only bothered to pull up his underwear before he sank to his knees between Drake's legs.

He took in Drake's package admiringly before taking his cock into his mouth. Garrett let his tongue swirl around the sensitive head and lap up the drops of pre-come that slipped from his slit. He traced the veins on the hard shaft, first with the tip of his tongue and then the flat, holding the root with his hand.

What Garrett lacked in technique, he made up for in enthusiasm. Drake guessed that Garrett hadn't given a lot of head, which meant a slow build.

"You don't have to take it all." Drake touched Garrett's cheek with his fingertips. "What you're doing is fine." He worried that Garrett was trying for a porn star performance with limited first-hand experience. "Just keep going," Drake coached. "Don't pause unless you're trying to give me blue balls. That's it. You don't have to be fancy. I'm feeling real good just with what you're doing. You'll get me there. I'm very sure." He gasped as Garrett's tongue swept over a sensitive spot.

True to his prediction, it didn't take long before Drake

felt his balls tighten and he came harder than usual, perhaps because of Garrett's inexperience. Or maybe just because it was Garrett earnestly worshiping his cock and giving it his best effort.

Garrett's eyes widened a bit, and then he managed to swallow.

"Next time, you can spit if you'd rather," Drake told him. "I won't be offended." He stretched behind him for the box of tissues he had seen on the nightstand, giving one to Garrett and using another to clean up before tucking himself in and pulling his underwear on. He left his jeans in a pile on the floor since he figured bed was the next stop.

"I just didn't want to disappoint you." Garrett blushed.

"Hey. Look at me." Drake tipped up Garrett's chin. "You aren't going to disappoint me because I want you however I can have you. I think it's kind of hot to learn new things together."

Garrett managed a smile as he put himself back together, putting his jeans to the side as well so that, like Drake, he was just in a T-shirt and briefs.

Drake held out a hand to him and lay back, wriggling to get them both on the bed even if they were atop the spread.

"That felt good," he told Garrett, knowing that giving head improved with repetition. "You'll find what works for you and makes it good for me. Just takes practice."

"I feel like I've missed out on some critical life skills," Garrett confessed. "Getting through vet school, interning, working in an emergency clinic, and then opening my own practice didn't leave a lot of free time. And honestly, I was so tired when I finally finished my shift that I didn't even jack off most nights. I can be pretty single-minded when I'm working on getting what I want."

Drake kissed him and pulled Garrett into his arms. "I

won't complain if you want to be single-minded about me," he teased. "I will happily enable that."

"Mmm. Sounds good." Sated and snuggled, Garrett looked adorably sleepy.

Drake let his hands explore Garrett's body, which was toned but not ripped. That made sense, he thought, since Garrett likely didn't have much time for the gym.

"I like touching you." Drake mapped the curves and angles with his palms and fingertips, not trying to arouse but to learn his lover's sensitive places. "And I like it when you touch me."

Drake hadn't been with an inexperienced lover in a long time, maybe since those fumbling firsts in high school. Some of his encounters had been a little too proficient for his liking, focused on technique over making an emotional connection because getting off was the only end game.

"I like touching you too," Garrett admitted it like a secret. "I want to know all the places that make you go crazy."

"That sounds like a great way to spend a weekend." Drake lightly kissed Garrett's shoulder to his neck. "I want to find out the same about you."

"I don't have a lot of stamina these days…it's been too long since I've gotten some on the regular. I did read that will improve with practice—I'd like to put that theory to the test." Garrett gave a wicked smile with a glint in his eyes.

"Oh, I'm very happy to help you practice." Drake leaned in to kiss him slow and sweet. "And there's no hurry. We can go at whatever pace you want. We only have to please ourselves."

Garrett looked down, suddenly nervous, and Drake frowned, wondering at the sudden shift. "Hey. What's wrong?" He crooked a finger under Garrett's chin and raised his head. "Talk to me."

"I know we've just started seeing each other," Garrett said.

"But I'm hoping that we can be…just us…while we figure out what this is between us."

"Exclusive?" Drake wanted to make sure he understood.

Garrett nodded. "Are you okay with that? Honestly, I'm not a play the field kind of guy. When I find something—or someone—I like, I tend to stick with it."

Drake pulled him into his arms and kissed him again. "I'm fine with that. And I have never been a notch in the bedpost type, either. Too much drama. I'm willing to see where this leads and take it day by day."

Garrett pulled him into a long, sweet kiss. Drake's cock twitched, but after his long day, he didn't think he would be ready for a second round before morning. One of the nice things about being out of his twenties was appreciating quality over quantity.

"We should probably clean up. It's late." Garrett drew back reluctantly. "I'll lay out a toothbrush for you—I have a bunch of them from dentist visits."

He gave Drake a peck on the tip of his nose and got out of bed, padding off to the bathroom while Drake pulled the covers down and folded the jeans he had left on the floor. While Garrett was in the bathroom, he glanced around the room, trying to get a sense of its owner without actively snooping.

An e-reader lay on the nightstand on what Drake assumed was Garrett's preferred side of the bed, next to an Arts and Crafts style table lamp and a box of tissues. The bedroom suite was real wood and actual furniture, not the flat packed assembly sort.

Framed photos on the top of the chest of drawers displayed what he guessed to be Garrett's family members on an outing at a lake. A few tchotchkes included an amethyst geode, a carved wooden dog, and a piece of pottery that looked hand-thrown.

Drake's job prized observation and analysis, and he couldn't turn that off, even in this setting. *Garrett values family. He's got a sentimental streak, so he likes souvenirs and things that remind him of special times. Maybe he inherited the bedroom furniture, but it's definitely a cut above the do-it-yourself stuff.*

That means he probably values creature comforts over just having a bunch of things. He realized that armchair psychology was often wrong, but he wanted to understand Garrett so he could give him what he needed.

Drake opened his senses, wanting a read from his psychic side. He fully believed Garrett was who he claimed to be and as he represented himself. Now, Drake wanted to understand his lover better.

Lover. I like the sound of that.

He listened with his gift, and impressions slowly filtered in. *Focused. Sentimental. Sincere. A little lonely. Family and friends matter to him. Kind—but nobody's pushover. Values the past. Optimistic. Ready to find someone.*

A few years ago, Drake might have been hesitant about a guy like Garrett who seemed too good to be true. But Drake had reached the point where he wanted more than work, even though he had become a secret agent like he had dreamed as a boy long ago. He wanted a person of his own, a home he shared with a lover—and maybe, a dog.

Bailey would do just fine.

"Your turn."

Garrett's voice jolted him from his thoughts. "Here," Garrett said. "Toothbrush and your very own mini-toothpaste."

"I think we're past the point of getting squeamish about sharing a toothpaste tube, don't you?" Drake snickered.

"Hey, just trying to be a good host," Garrett joked. "I'm out of practice."

Drake stood and pulled him into his arms. "I'll make sure you get plenty of practice," he murmured, ending with a kiss.

"I like the sound of that."

Garrett had changed into a pair of thin drawstring sleep pants that did little to conceal his ass or his package. Drake's cock approved, and he made plans to have a very happy morning.

"Do you mind if I just sleep in my briefs? I didn't bring anything else."

"I don't mind at all," Garrett said with an exaggerated, lecherous grin. "And if you want, bring an extra pair of sleep pants next time, and you can leave them here."

"I only brought one pair since I'm living out of a suitcase for the moment," Drake reminded him. "But I can definitely do that once I go back to my apartment."

"Oh, right." Garrett's smile dimmed as he turned away. Drake caught him by the shoulder and pulled him back.

"Spill. What's on your mind?"

Garrett sighed. "I just—the last time I tried a distance relationship, back in college, it didn't go well. I guess I pushed it out of my mind that you don't live here in Moundsville."

Drake pushed Garett's hair back from his face. "I've got a place on the close end of Wheeling, and as you pointed out, it's not far. Down the line, if it's a problem, maybe we look for somewhere in between. I don't go into the office most days, so it's less of an issue for me."

"I'm getting the cart before the horse." Garrett sighed. "It's what I do best."

"Hey, don't trash talk my boyfriend." The word sent a thrill through him and seemed to have the same effect on Garrett.

"I'll try not to," Garrett replied with a shy grin. To Drake's surprise, Garrett gave him a slap on the ass. "Go get ready for bed. I'll take Bailey out. That's part of why I don't sleep in my skivvies." He hesitated. "He's used to sleeping in the same room with me, but not on the bed." He nodded toward a large dog pillow in the corner.

"I'm just the guest. I'm not going to do anything to make Bailey uncomfortable in his own home." Drake was privately glad that the pooch—nice as he was—wouldn't be sharing the mattress.

"For what it's worth, I think Bailey likes you," Garrett said. "I...kinda have a sense about these things."

Drake tilted his head, looking more closely. His intuition hadn't pinged on a strong psychic ability in Garrett, but what he had originally thought was considerable empathy he now realized might be a touch of something extra.

"You can communicate with him?"

Garrett looked a little uncomfortable. "Not like in words. Every good vet reads animal body language. I just go a little beyond that, where it's not like I carry on a conversation, but I pick up on feelings and emotions more than maybe the average pet owner."

"That probably comes in handy, being a vet."

"Most of the time, yes. But sometimes...I wish I didn't. Those are the bad days." He looked so sad, Drake pulled him close again and held him tightly.

"I didn't mean to upset you."

Garrett shook his head, still nestled against Drake's shoulder. "You didn't know. And like I said, most of the time it helps me calm them down if they're uncomfortable or scared. But the other times...it can be rough."

"It sounds like you're a really good vet—and a great pet parent," Drake said. "Speaking of which—go take care of Bailey before he decides that I'm a nuisance and pees on my shoes."

Drake cleaned up and returned to the bedroom, feeling a

little unsure. By then, Garrett had taken care of Bailey and was already in bed. He seemed to sense his uncertainty and lifted the covers, indicating for Drake to join him. Drake smiled and slid in beside him.

"I don't have to go into the clinic until ten tomorrow," Garrett said. "The staff will open and take care of the things that don't need an actual doctor. So we can get things off to a good start." His smile suggested that he had round two in mind.

Drake kissed him. "I like the sound of that."

The room was too warm for snuggling, but Drake liked the way Garrett kept a hand barely touching him, a tether as they fell asleep. Drake breathed in Garrett's scent that surrounded him—soap, shampoo, laundry detergent, and musk. Despite the case and its loose ends, Drake fell asleep soundly for the first time in a long while.

It couldn't last.

Drake saw an abandoned warehouse dimly lit and fallen into disrepair. He caught the unmistakable smell of pharmaceutical chemicals and knew he had found the witch's lab.

Bodies littered the floor, adding the stink of blood to the tang in the air. Some had bullet holes, but other corpses bore clear evidence that magic had been involved.

Charred metal and broken glass testified to a battle. If this was where the witch cabal produced its paranormal pharmaceuticals, then there had been a hell of a fight here, both magical and mundane.

Shards crunched beneath his boots as he walked amid the carnage. He didn't recognize any of the dead, but many had been burned and mangled beyond identification.

Drake gripped his gun, taking comfort from its familiar weight in his hand. He stopped and listened, but the only sound was the lonesome howl of the wind wailing through the broken roof.

What he saw didn't add up. Dead workers, broken equipment—but where was the product?

Whoever did the killing took the drugs.

Or else they got rid of inconvenient people and staged the site to put him off the trail.

Tendrils of dark and malicious magic swarmed around him, trying to break through his protections. Whoever killed these people knew Drake would find them, left this to send a message, mocking him and daring him to chase them.

"It isn't over yet."

"Drake! Drake, wake up!" Garrett's panicked voice roused Drake from the vision.

Drake came back to himself, breathing hard and sweat-soaked.

"Are you okay?" Garrett's eyes were wide with fear.

"Yeah. Fuck. Yeah, I'm okay. I'm okay," Drake repeated, not sure whether he was trying to convince himself or Garrett. Things might not actually happen in real life like his dream, but Drake had learned to heed the warning of his visions even if the particulars differed.

"What happened? Do you need a doctor?"

Drake shook his head. "Nothing a doctor can do." He managed a wan smile. "Not even a cute veterinarian."

"Not funny."

Drake sighed. He had hoped to put off this conversation longer, but he knew Garrett wouldn't be dissuaded.

"I told you that I'm psychic. That's part of my government job. I get visions. I don't control when or what they're about. Sometimes they're related to my case, and other times they might be a warning for someone I know, but that isn't work related—like having a car accident." His words tumbled out in a rush, and he didn't try to meet Garrett's eyes.

"I see things that might happen, but that future can still be changed. Except I don't know which type of vision is which until later," Drake finished.

"Does it hurt?" Garrett had switched to professional mode, patting him down, assessing his eyes, doing a quick triage.

Drake shook his head. "No. Just...it's very real when I'm in the vision. More than a regular nightmare. And it's a glimpse of what the future 'could' be, but that isn't fixed. It can be changed, but I don't know what to do to change it."

"Doesn't sound like much help." Garrett got up and returned with a glass of water, which Drake gulped down.

He handed back the glass and shook his head when Garrett offered a refill.

"No, thanks. I just need to sit for a bit."

Garrett reached for the pulse point in Drake's neck. "Take some deep breaths before you pass out."

They were quiet for several moments as Drake got his breathing under control, and his heart rate gradually slowed.

"That's better." Garrett gave him a clinical once-over as he took Drake's pulse again. "This is not the kind of doctor that's fun to play."

"I'm sorry."

Garrett shook his head. "Nothing to apologize for. It's part of getting to know each other—although they never covered this in the dating columns I've read."

"Maybe you should read Psychic's Weekly," Drake joked, making up a title on the spot.

"Maybe." Garrett still looked worried. "What did you see?"

Drake paused, trying to figure out what to say. "I think it had to do with the case I'm working on, the situation that brought me to Moundsville. There was an abandoned warehouse, and people were dead. But I think someone was using the warehouses illegally, and it went wrong in a big way."

He didn't want to drag Garrett into his case or put him at risk. At the same time, he owed him some explanation after putting on a show like that in bed.

"There are a lot of warehouses down by the river," Garrett said. "Some are clearly still in use, but there are others that don't look like anyone has used them in a long time. Most people around here steer clear of that area. It attracts a rough sort. Be careful if you go there. I know you're a fed, but the danger is real."

"What do people say?" Drake's heart still pounded, but his brain was coming back online after the swell of panic subsided.

Garrett shrugged. "Some people say it's drugs. Others say there are thieves who store and sell what they steal—and don't like being interrupted. So if you go down there, take backup and go armed."

"Thanks," Drake replied but didn't promise.

"You know, even tough-guy secret agents can ask for a hug after a bad vision," Garrett said, giving Drake absolution and understanding with his gaze.

Drake let Garrett's arms enfold him, resting his head on Garrett's shoulder, letting his new boyfriend be the strong one for once.

"I'm sorry. This isn't helping you get any sleep."

"Pfft. Sleeping is overrated," Garrett joked. "It's okay to ask for comfort—even for big, bad federal agents."

"Not something I've got much experience with," Drake confessed. "But I can see the appeal."

"Can you get backup? Surely they don't expect you to nab all the bad guys by yourself."

Drake sighed and disentangled himself, pulling them both down to lie close together.

"Yes, I can call in backup—and I will, once I have a better idea of what's going on and who's involved." He tangled his fingers in Garrett's hair. "Sorry for being vague, but the less you know, the safer you are."

"Okay," Garrett said softly. "I have to trust your judgment. But please—don't take crazy chances."

"That's kinda my job."

Garrett fixed him with a glare. "Don't be stupid about it, then. I like having you around, and I would be deeply pissed if you got hurt."

"Doctor's orders?" Drake grinned, trying to lighten the mood.

"Do you realize that a veterinarian is permitted to treat and prescribe for immediate family members? So yes, if that's what it takes to get you to be careful."

Drake pulled Garrett closer and kissed him. "I'll do the best I can. That's the most I can promise. But I've got plenty of new incentives." He kissed Garrett again.

Garrett looked at the bedside clock and groaned. "Ugh. I'm going to have to get up before too long. Let's see if we can get back to sleep until then."

That didn't prove too difficult for Garrett, who was lightly snoring minutes later, one arm flung over Drake's waist.

Drake lay awake for a while, still trying to figure out the meaning of his vision. He had learned that while the superficial purposes usually seemed clear, there was often a second, deeper meaning that didn't become obvious sometimes until hindsight.

Tomorrow, I'll look for the warehouse. But is it a clue about the drugs, the shifter trafficking, or a warning that isn't so literal?

He wracked his brain to figure out a metaphorical meaning and came up empty.

Let's assume it's a vision connected to the case. Something big went down in one of the empty warehouses, and it either hasn't hit the news, hasn't been discovered, or hasn't happened yet, but it might.

His visions sometimes showed him possible outcomes that could still change, not foregone conclusions. So that might mean he could stop the slaughter if he could figure out what the vision wanted him to know.

It could be a hand-off place for the paranormal drugs and some sort of rival shootout happened. Or a deal gone bad for trafficked shifters or psychics. But without more to go on, I can't tell what led to the killings or which factions are at war.

And if this does give me a crack in the case, I may need to step back from Garrett for a little while for his own safety.

That thought made him sad, but he knew he couldn't live with himself if Garrett got hurt because of him.

I'll go have a look down on the riverfront, see if I can figure out what's going on.

Tomorrow, I'll go looking for trouble.

CHAPTER FIVE

GARRETT

*I*n the morning, Garrett and Drake made love slowly, sleepy hand jobs in bed and then another round of blow jobs in the shower.

"I could get very used to waking up like this," he teased as they showered away the jizz and sweat.

"I'm in favor." Drake leaned in for a water-soaked kiss.

As they toweled off, Garrett thought back to their lovemaking the night before. "I'm sorry that I'm not ready yet to try more new positions," he blurted, giving voice to the worry that had been gnawing at him.

He knew he was inexperienced. Drake had been patient and hadn't pushed, and their relationship was still very new. *But how long will he wait for me to catch up? I don't want to disappoint him, but I also don't want to do anything I'm not comfortable doing.*

Drake rested his hands on Garrett's shoulders and looked him in the eye. "Where's this coming from? I thought we did pretty well by each other last night—and that was one of the best showers I've had in my life just now."

Garrett couldn't help feeling self-conscious. "I just don't want to disappoint you because we haven't done anal."

Drake pushed a wet strand of hair out of Garrett's face. "You know, some people never do it, and that's okay. Yes, it can feel amazing, giving and receiving. I'd like to share that with you. But only when you're ready. And if it isn't something you ever want to do...we can come up with a lot of other ways to get off and feel good."

Garrett wanted to believe him, but he still worried. "I tried it once," he confessed. "In college. It...didn't go well."

Drake cupped Garrett's face with his hand. "That means your partner didn't know what he was doing and didn't prep you right. Good prep makes all the difference, and it can be arousing as hell just getting ready. If you decide you want to try it, I can make it good for you. And if you don't—it's not going to make me leave."

"Promise?" Garrett felt young and vulnerable despite being a doctor in his thirties.

"Promise."

Garrett's medical training gave him more than enough knowledge to figure out how human anatomy worked for anal sex. He had read articles on how to do it right, without discomfort, so both partners could enjoy the experience. Unfortunately, after that early bad encounter, Garrett had used being busy as an excuse to stick with other, less fraught, ways of giving and receiving pleasure.

"I just thought I should say so up front in case it changed anything." Garrett tried not to let his insecurities show. Despite it being early days together, he had already figured out that he was falling fast and hard.

Drake kissed him again. "It doesn't change a thing. We have lots of options. But most of all, I just want you, any way I can have you."

"Thank you," Garrett said and meant *I think I could love you.*

It seemed far too early to say that out loud. Garrett worried that his strong feelings might seem like inexperience, and he knew he probably hadn't done as much as Drake or most men his age. He didn't want to scare Drake off by admitting too much, too soon. And in the back of his mind, although Garrett knew it was ridiculous, he worried a little that his secret agent boyfriend had James Bond's experience in bed.

"I'm not a spy, and I don't sleep with everything that moves," Drake teased, and Garrett realized he had forgotten about his boyfriend's psychic abilities.

"I didn't mean—"

Drake kissed him again and gave him an indulgent look. "Of course you did. Those movies are completely unrealistic. And even if they weren't, that's not me. Let's take this one step at a time and see where we end up, huh?"

"I'm good with that," Garrett replied.

Once they were dressed, Garrett fried eggs while Drake managed toast and the coffee maker. They worked around each other efficiently, even though it was Drake's first time navigating Garrett's space.

"You're already a good influence," Drake said as they sat down to eat. "I usually grab a toaster pastry on the way out the door."

Garrett didn't have to fake a shudder. "It's a miracle you're still alive. Good food doesn't have to take a long time to make. If I know I'm going to be swamped, I do up a dozen hardboiled eggs, and that way, I can grab and go."

"You're going to help me change my ways for the better; I can already tell," Drake joked.

After breakfast, Drake gathered his things to head out.

Garrett found himself hoping that their relationship would move forward to living together so they didn't have to say goodbye.

Don't rush it. If it's meant to be, it'll happen in its own time, he told himself, but found it difficult to take the advice to heart.

"Don't forget—we have a date tonight." Drake pulled Garrett in for a goodbye kiss.

"I'm counting on it. Can you stay over again?"

"Yes—as long as it's okay if I leave earlier. I need to take care of some things and get an early start."

"I am capable of using an alarm clock," Garrett teased. "We can totally make that happen."

Drake stole another kiss and gave Garrett's ass a squeeze, then headed out. Garrett barely kept himself from watching out the window, deciding that was entirely too sappy, although he wanted to watch until Drake was out of sight.

I've got it bad.

Garrett fed Bailey and took him out for a walk. "I hope you like Drake because I'm pretty smitten," he confessed as they headed down the block.

Bailey wagged his tail and gave him a goofy look, which Garrett chose to interpret as positive. "Just think—double the petting, twice the treats, and lots of fetch."

Garrett had been relieved when Drake took to Bailey because he knew that if they hadn't gotten along, it would have been a deal-breaker. *Thank God he's a dog lover.*

He took Bailey for a little longer walk than usual to make up for him having to share his attention with Drake. At one point, he thought a burgundy sedan followed him, but then it turned off, and he chalked his worry up to paranoia.

If I'm going to fall for a fed, I'm going to have to get used to a little more risk, for him and me. We'll figure it out. Other agents make it work—so can we. Garrett crossed his fingers on that since all he knew about federal agents he learned from watching television.

Once they got home, Garrett made the bed, tidied up after breakfast, and changed for work. He got Bailey into his car harness and headed for the clinic, keeping a slightly paranoid eye on the rearview mirror in case the sedan showed up again.

He made it to the clinic without spotting the burgundy sedan and convinced himself that he had watched too many detective movies. Even so, he carefully scanned the parking lot before he and Bailey got out of the SUV.

From the cars that he knew didn't belong to his staff, it looked like the morning had gotten off to a busy start.

"Everything okay?" he asked as he walked past the front desk with Bailey. He saw several people already in the waiting room.

"We had a bunch of prescription refills and nail trims," Patty told him, "You're booked for vaccinations and annual physicals for most of the morning. I printed your schedule, and it's on your desk along with the charts I pulled."

"I couldn't survive without you," Garrett told her, meaning every word.

Garrett changed into scrubs and looked over his appointments. The afternoon held several sick visits, a new puppy examination, and wellness checks for two senior dogs.

He checked his phone occasionally but didn't expect to hear from Drake during the workday, especially since they had just been together and would see each other that evening. Between patients, Garrett found his mind wandering, looking forward to their date that evening.

"Something on your mind, Doc?" Kirsten asked, and Garrett realized he must have zoned out waiting for the next patient to come to the treatment room.

"Nothing wrong. Just thinking about the weekend," he fibbed. His office staff were close, but he wasn't ready to say anything about his relationship until things weren't quite so new between him and Drake. While Garrett thought all the signs certainly pointed toward good luck, he tried to keep his personal life private until the point where introductions might be necessary.

Since he had basically no personal life to speak of since he started the clinic, that hadn't been too hard.

"Doing something fun besides working?" Kirsten asked.

"Maybe. We'll see how the weather is, but I've been thinking of going on some of the trails over at Grand Vue."

The state park offered hiking trails, but it also had geocaching and disc golf. It was one of Bailey's favorite spots, and Garrett was hoping he could introduce Drake to it as well.

"It's nice over there," she replied. "I haven't been in a while—it always seems to rain on my days off—but it's a pretty place and fairly quiet most of the time."

Garrett realized he had no idea whether Drake liked or merely tolerated the outdoors. While he wasn't a true wilderness enthusiast—he preferred motels to tents— Garrett found that exploring several nearby state parks was calming after a busy week at work. Bailey enjoyed the outings and they both benefited from the exercise and time in nature.

"Bailey likes doing some of the easier hikes," Garrett said. "I think he has fun seeing all the birds and squirrels, even if he can't chase them."

"Smart dog. I should go to the parks more often," Kirsten admitted. "I get busy running errands, and poof—the weekend is gone."

The sick visits turned out to be uncomplicated, something Garrett never took for granted. He loved being able to help a pet feel better, and even after all these years, he took it nearly as hard as the owner when he had to give bad news.

"You liked the puppy, didn't you, Bailey?" Garrett said after they finished the exam, and Pepper, a young beagle, left with her owner. "I think she'd give you a run for your money. But you're the only dog for me." He ruffled Bailey's ears.

The first wellness check went fine. But on the second, Garrett had to share bad news.

"Daisy will be fine for a while," he told Mrs. Castille, the dog's owner, while gently petting the older dog's head. "But be prepared for a sudden turn for the worse. She's at that age when a number of things could go wrong out of the blue, and when that happens, it tends to trigger other weak points. They can go pretty fast."

"I understand," Mrs. Castille said, cradling Daisy, a Pekingese, in her lap. "I've been grateful for every year we've had together, but I knew the clock was ticking. She's not in pain, is she?"

Garrett shook his head, and Mrs. Castille visibly relaxed. "No. I would have told you. For now, she's doing great. Watch for any changes in habits or behavior. Just enjoy every day. Spoil her a little. Let me know if anything changes."

Mrs. Castille gathered the dog into her arms. "Thank you so much, Dr. Thompson. You always take such good care of my Daisy."

Garrett managed a frozen smile until the door closed, and he passed a hand over his eyes.

"It's not going to be long, is it?" Kirsten asked. He knew she had enough experience to see the old dog's symptoms for what they were.

"No. And I know Daisy is in her nineties in people years, and she's had a wonderful life. But...it's always too soon," Garrett said.

He took a few moments in the break room to pull himself

together. Helping pets and their owners through illness and end of life was part of his job, and he approached it with the reverence of clergy. Still, it never got easier.

"Hey, boss." Kirsten stuck her head in. "Can I get you anything?"

Garrett blinked hard and shook his head. "No. I'm okay. It's just the part of the job I hate the most."

"I know," Kirsten agreed. "But look at it this way—you'll make it as easy as you can for both Mrs. Castille and Daisy. That's a blessing."

"Yeah. I tell myself that. But it never gets easier."

"I don't think it's supposed to when you do it right."

He managed a watery smile. "Thanks."

Bailey seemed to sense Garrett's mood. He wound through the clinic's back hallway to find him and bumped against his leg, wanting ear scratches.

"Thanks, boy." Garrett knelt next to Bailey and wrapped his arms around the dog. "You always know what I need." He hugged Bailey until Kirsten knocked on the doorframe to let him know the next patient had arrived.

"Extra treats tonight for being my emotional support dog," Garrett promised Bailey, pulling a treat out of his pocket for him. "Good boy."

Fortunately, the rest of the afternoon passed quickly. None of the sick visits were anything serious; nothing antibiotics and food changes wouldn't fix.

As they were getting ready to close for the night, Garett dropped by the front desk. "Anything from Mr. Colletta?"

Patty shook her head. "No. Were you expecting to hear from him?"

Really hoping we never hear from him again. "Not really. I just wondered—he seemed very worried about his dog."

"I guess even tough guys have a soft spot for someone,"

Patty replied, which Garrett took to be a diplomatic way to say, "Even gangsters love their dogs."

Garrett tried to focus on the positives as he changed back to street clothes. The rest of the animals he had treated that day didn't have serious conditions and would make a full recovery. They were doted upon by owners who loved them. And the pets definitely returned the affection.

Sometimes Garrett thought the owners were as much his patients as the pets since they often mentioned the things going on in their lives that affected the situation. He wasn't qualified as a people doctor or a therapist, but he knew, beyond questioning, that the bond between pet and owner contributed greatly to good health and happiness for both of them.

"Come on, Bailey. Let's go home and get you fed and taken care of," he said as Bailey wagged happily on the way to the SUV.

"You're such a good boy." He talked to Bailey on the drive home to take his mind off the day. "What do you think of Drake? He likes you. I bet he'd bring you all kinds of treats if you'd put in a good word for him."

Bailey yipped, and Garrett couldn't tell whether it was a sympathetic response to his tone or he had spotted birds in the trees by the road. He chose to take it as support.

"I like him a lot," Garrett confided. "Like, a lot a lot. Is that wrong? I know we just started seeing each other. And I wasn't really actually *looking* for someone, although I'd thought it would be nice to find the right person. And then there he was."

He glanced at Bailey in the rearview mirror. He was staring out the side window, tongue hanging out, happily grinning.

"Do you think you could get used to having him around

all the time? Because I'm falling pretty hard for him. That way, you could have two papas. Would you like that?"

I'm discussing my love life with my dog. Then again, who knows me better?

Garrett let Bailey out to romp in the backyard before calling him inside and feeding him dinner. He nibbled some crackers and cheese while Bailey ate so he wouldn't be famished when Drake arrived and tidied up the house since he was planning to bring Drake back here after their date.

After Bailey was settled, Garrett took a shower, once again cleaning down there so he was ready no matter what direction the night took.

Maybe I should look into a butt plug. That way I could get used to the feeling of being...open. It might make me less nervous when we get to the real thing.

I'm more nervous about the unknown than whether it will be uncomfortable at first. I trust Drake, even though we haven't known each other long. I think he'd make it good for me. But that would probably be easier if I wasn't a nervous wreck.

He appreciated Drake's patience with moving the physical side of their relationship to the next level, and he understood that they had options for intimacy. Garrett had always imagined that he would eventually at least try anal again. Reading about it in romance books and watching explicit videos definitely were a turn-on. He hoped it would be something he could share with Drake and tried to be patient with himself.

I'm not exactly a thirty-three-year-old virgin, but sometimes I feel like it. It's not like I was saving myself. I didn't like how it went the time I tried, and I don't want to have that happen again.

But Drake's not like that. I'm sure he has more experience than I do—everyone does. I don't like thinking about him with other partners, but we're exclusive now, and I'll benefit from what he's learned.

We've got time. He's not rushing me. I'll relax as we get to know each other.

I have to believe that everything will work out.

Drake knocked on the door a few minutes before six-thirty. A rust-brown shirt brought out the color in his eyes, and Garrett liked the way Drake's slim-cut jeans clung to his ass and thighs.

"Ready for the adventure?" Drake grinned.

"We'd better get moving because those jeans make me think of a whole different sort of adventure," Garrett confessed.

"The good news—we can do both."

Garrett locked the door and followed Drake to his truck. "I thought we'd catch dinner first, then round two for the escape room and mini-golf," Drake said. "We can do billiards and bowling later—or save it for another time. Sound okay to you?"

"Sounds great. I'm starved."

Drake pulled up in front of a diner, one that looked like an old trolley car. "I haven't eaten here yet, but everyone told me it was really good," he said. "It's not fancy, but I hear the pie is amazing."

"Your intel is spot-on. Wayside Diner is a classic," Garrett replied. "I've been meaning to try it. And I heard the same thing about their milkshakes."

"I read that the whole thing about looking like train cars was because the early diners were pre-fabricated, and making them into a railroad car made them easy to ship," Drake said. "Now they're nostalgic. I've always thought they were cool—and they do usually have amazing food."

The interior of the diner played up its mid-century roots, with jukeboxes at each table and classic server uniforms. They found a table near the back and settled in. Garrett took a deep breath, taking in the scent of chili and burgers, and his stomach rumbled.

"Looks like we got here just in time before you expired from hunger," Drake joked.

Garrett gave a sheepish grin. "It was a busy day. I kinda ate lunch on the run."

The menu seemed to have a little of everything since the diner was open around the clock. Drake ordered a cheeseburger and fries with a vanilla milkshake. Garrett opted for a breakfast serving of hash browns, fried eggs, and bacon, with coffee and a slice of cherry pie.

"I might be in a food coma when we're done," Garrett admitted. "The portions look generous." He nodded in the direction of the nearby tables.

"Fuel for the adventure to come," Drake said, smiling. "How was your day?"

"Pretty good. Not very exciting. No emergencies. Everyone walked out better than when they showed up, so that's a win in my book," Garrett replied. "And my least favorite patient didn't show up, so that's something."

"How did he get on the naughty list? Did he bite you?"

Garrett shook his head, feeling bad that he had brought up the subject since he hadn't meant to dim the mood. "Just a jerk of an owner. The dog is fine. Dogs usually are. Sometimes people suck."

"That's the truth," Drake agreed.

Heaping plates filled with steaming food appeared before they had much chance to talk.

"This smells even better than it looks, and it looks awesome," Garrett said when the server put their meals on the table. "I might not need to eat for a week if I finish this."

"I can think of fun ways to burn calories," Drake said in a low voice, raising an eyebrow to get his point across. Garrett felt himself chub in his jeans.

"So can I—and I'm counting on it," he flirted back.

Neither of them picked jukebox songs, but the tables around them kept the tunes coming. Drake nudged his knee under the table, and Garrett felt like a high schooler with a crush.

The pie and milkshake were just as good as expected, and by the time they finished eating, Garrett needed activity to avoid falling asleep.

"Since we had a good time at the arcade last time, I found a different escape room and mini golf for tonight. I thought we could hit the escape room first," Garrett said since it had been his turn to set up the date. "And maybe next time, if the weather is good, we could try the trails at Grand Vue Park."

"Another escape room, huh?" Drake asked.

Garrett shook his head. "It was fun last time, and this one is supposed to be more challenging."

They picked a different haunted mansion setting, and since this was date night, Garrett had reserved a time for just the two of them instead of having to be part of a larger group. The guide explained the rules, made sure they understood the time limit, and sent them into the themed room.

Drake caught his eye, turned his back to the camera that let the game-runners watch the participants, and partially withdrew a small leather case from the inside pocket of his jacket.

"Is that—?" Garrett thought he recognized a lock pick kit from a show he'd watched.

Drake nodded, and Garrett remembered in time that the rooms had mics and cameras to help the players and also make sure nothing inappropriate happened.

"I guess that's a bit of insurance."

"We're starting out conscious and not tied up, so I'm counting that as a win."

Maybe bringing a federal agent to an escape room wasn't the best idea.

Drake grinned. "It's pretend, just like going to a scary movie. I like it much better this way."

A stoic man in a formal butler's uniform introduced himself as their guide and ushered them to the antechamber.

"Welcome to Harbinger Hall," the man intoned. "Tonight, you have been invited as guests of the Duke of Harbinger for a dinner party. But when you arrive at the mansion, you find it deserted. Where have the guests gone? Is this a prank, or something much more nefarious? What about the Duke? Is he in on the joke, or has he also been spirited away?"

Their guide paused. "And speaking of spirits...do they really haunt the halls of this old mansion? Are they trying to warn you—or trying to stop you from solving the Haunting of Harbinger Hall? You have sixty minutes to find the clues, solve the mystery, and unlock the door to free you from the adventure," he continued, no longer as dramatic.

"We can see and hear you. If you have questions, speak up. Don't damage any of the props. Things you are meant to find will be findable without harming the room or the items. The door is not locked, but leaving ends the adventure. Please keep your phones turned off and out of sight. That's it! Have fun—and may you get the best of the Haunting of Harbinger Hall."

With that, their guide opened the door, ushered them inside, and closed it behind them.

"Wow." Garrett took in the elaborate Victorian parlor. "This looks like something out of Scooby-Doo."

"I was thinking *Clue*, the movie, but okay," Drake agreed.

Garrett and Drake each took a side of the room to search. Garrett quickly realized that while Drake gamely played along and seemed to be having fun, he didn't seem to be concentrating very hard and let Garrett take the lead.

"It never occurred to me that this might be a lot like your day job," Garrett said after they successfully swept the first room and found both a key and a note, directing them to the locked inner chamber.

Drake put a finger over his lips, and Garrett got the message—*Don't spill the beans about the secret agent stuff.*

"Hey—they've done a great job with the set and the plot," Drake pointed out. "It's not smelly and rat-infested or lousy with asbestos. Those are all definite improvements. I wish everything was like this."

Drake hung back and let Garrett take the lead, chiming in when Garrett asked for help and occasionally nudging him toward well-hidden clues.

Working together felt comfortable, even if Drake wasn't putting in his full effort. Garrett appreciated that Drake played along and let him enjoy the adventure. When they solved the mystery in forty-five minutes instead of the allotted sixty, they won a gift certificate, and each got a button reading "Escape Artist."

They walked out, and Garrett turned to Drake. "You figured it out early."

"Finding the answer wasn't really the point," Drake said. "It was the process that was supposed to be fun."

"Thanks for not spoiling it." Garrett was impressed. Lots of guys would have used the chance to show off, even when they weren't a government agent.

"Hey, it's a lot more fun when no one's really trying to kill you." Drake held out his wrists. "No rope burn. No headache from getting pistol-whipped. And no real ghosts. Those are all big pluses in my book."

"I hope you weren't bored." Garrett worried that Drake didn't have a good time.

Drake reached over and gave his hand a quick squeeze. "I'm with you. Of course I enjoyed it. And remember—a script has to make sense. What I deal with might have a certain logic to the perpetrator, but that doesn't always add up for someone who isn't—"

"Bonkers," Garrett supplied.

"Effectively—yes. Although that's not a textbook term," Drake agreed with a grin. "I thought the room was very creative—and a lot more fun than the real thing."

"I'm glad because we've got a gift certificate, and Bailey only works for dog treats," Garrett joked. "Still up for mini-golf?"

"Sure. The evening's still young," Drake agreed. "We can play golf—and go back to your place for a hole-in-one." He gave an exaggerated leer.

Every time Garrett didn't think he could fall harder, Drake did something unexpectedly wonderful that just made him even more smitten.

I never thought I could feel so much, so fast. Taking this slow is going to be rough.

Two black-light-themed mini-golf courses presented a choice—Alien Encounter or Killer in the Cornfield.

"I vote for aliens," Drake said. "At least I don't deal with them at work. That's another department."

Garrett looked at him, trying to decide whether Drake was joking.

"You're kidding, right?"

Drake shrugged. "The truth is out there."

"Very *X-Files*." *And managing not to confirm or deny.*

The glowing course wound through flying saucers, little green men, pyramids, crop circles, and strange statues with alien hieroglyphics. Everything glowed under the black lights, including their clothing.

"Someone put a lot into this course." Drake gestured to the blinking lights and props. "I like it."

Garrett pointed toward the ceiling, where a cow statue

was being lifted by a glowing tractor beam into a silver spaceship.

"That's what no one talks about," Drake joked. "Alien cow tipping. Pretty sure I saw it on one of those ancient astronaut shows."

Garrett was pleased that they were more evenly matched at golf, and he didn't feel like Drake was holding back. Neither of them was likely to make the pro circuit, but they had a good time laughing at the elaborate decorations that recreated iconic sci-fi movie scenes.

"Tied—and not in a bad way," Garrett proclaimed as they sank the last hole.

"Personally, I prefer handcuffs," Drake said with a naughty wink that sent heat low in Garrett's belly.

"I'll remember that." He was no longer sure when Drake was teasing and felt his cheeks heat.

They did well enough to score half-off coupons for a return visit. "Next time, I'd like to do the Ancient Pyramids course," Garrett said. "It looked fun."

"So did the Voodoo Bayou course," Drake said. "And there's still billiards and bowling. I guess this means more dates, huh?"

"Are you in it just for the mini-golf?" Garrett joked.

"If I said it was because of your great ass, would you hold it against me?"

"Absolutely not." Garrett was glad he'd chosen this pair of jeans because they definitely showed his assets off to advantage.

Garrett noticed that Drake seemed wary crossing the parking lot and glanced in the rearview mirror often as he drove. *Maybe being over-cautious just goes with the job.* "Are you worried about something?"

Drake smiled, but it didn't reach his eyes, and he still had what Garrett thought of as his on duty look.

"I'm in town on a case. I don't know how much the bad guys know or whether they realize I'm on their tail. I don't want to put you in any danger."

Garrett sensed Drake's strong protective streak and didn't want to have him decide that he needed to walk away for Garrett's sake.

"Hey. I appreciate caution, but I'm a grown-ass man, and I get a say in the risks I take," Garrett said. "I like you a lot. I know you have to go back to Wheeling when you're done with the case, but I've already figured out the best routes to visit. Which means that working around the dangers of your job is going to be part of making this thing between us last."

"I don't want to put you on the radar of bad people who might want to hurt you to get to me." Drake didn't look away from the road as he spoke, but Garrett got the feeling he had already given the risk too much thought.

"I know people whose partners are cops and soldiers and firefighters," Garrett countered. "All dangerous professions. But that doesn't stop people from falling in love and making relationships work. It can be done—if we want it badly enough."

Drake didn't take his eyes off the road. "I already know that I want this."

Garrett's heart soared, but he dug in his heels. "Then we have to figure out how to fight for it. Because I'm not afraid."

Drake reached over and took his hand. "That's okay—I'll worry enough for both of us."

When they got to Garrett's house, Drake volunteered to take Bailey out. Garrett figured that gave Drake an opportunity to make sure no one was lurking while Bailey got to do business.

Garrett turned on music as he fixed a snack tray of salami, cheese, crackers, and olives and poured them both glasses of wine. After the party atmosphere of the escape room and mini-golf, he needed a chance to shift to romance.

He chided himself for overthinking like a high schooler on a first date. Earlier, he stashed a tube of lube in the drawer of the end table by the couch and made sure lube and condoms were in the nightstand.

All evening the sexual tension fairly crackled between them. Garrett had been half-hard since dinner from proximity and in anticipation of where the evening might go. But most importantly, even if they didn't end up doing more than making out, he'd had a great time just being together, which counted for a lot.

One of the reasons Garrett had shied away from dating was how strained those evenings often felt. Either it seemed like they were rushing through dinner and a movie expecting to end up in bed, or the chemistry just wasn't present.

With Drake, Garrett felt red-hot attraction, but he could still enjoy having an evening out without feeling like it was all just a prelude to sex.

That's got to be a good sign, right? We can't stay in bed forever.

He had seen other couples who seemed utterly combustible together flame out after a few months because all they had was sexual attraction. Garrett had always hoped he would find someone with a mix of sex appeal and shared interests so they could go the distance. Deep inside, he wanted to find his forever man—and the more he was around Drake, the more Garrett hoped he had already found what he was looking for.

They'd had a busy evening, but since they started early it wasn't as late as Garrett originally thought, which meant time for hijinks and still getting enough sleep to function in the morning.

"Bailey has thoroughly checked your yard and found it

squirrel-free," Drake reported when he and Bailey came inside. "You can rest easy."

Bailey bounded up to Garrett, who ruffled his fur and ears. "Bailey's a good boy, aren't you?"

He looked up to see Drake looking fondly at Bailey. "I always wanted a dog," he admitted. "But my mom was allergic, and then I had jobs that didn't lend themselves to being home enough. So I appreciate being able to borrow Bailey."

If you decide to keep me, you get Bailey as a bonus.

"I think he's smitten with you," Garrett said. *And so am I.*

Drake moved in close and took Garrett in his arms. "He's not the only one who's smitten." His voice dropped into that lower register that made Garrett even hornier.

"Oh, yeah?"

"Uh-huh." Drake kissed Garrett, long and slow, tangling one hand in his hair and gripping his ass with the other.

"Maybe we should do something about that," Garrett replied, already a little breathless.

"Oh, we definitely should." He jerked his head toward the charcuterie. "Why don't you put that in the fridge for later. Bailey might seize the moment while I've got you distracted."

"That sounds like a good idea." Garrett disentangled himself and put the tray in the refrigerator. He gave a yelp when Drake came up behind him and nibbled on his ear.

"You taste good. Can I snack on you?"

Several risqué replies came to mind, but his brain short-circuited before he could say them out loud as Drake's tongue traced the shell of his ear.

Garrett managed to close the fridge door and turn in Drake's arms. Before he could react, Drake picked him up and put him on the counter making up for the height difference between them. "Nice to see eye to eye."

God, that's hot.

"I think you liked that." Drake's lips were close to his ear as one hand slid between Garrett's legs. "Pretty sure, actually."

"Bedroom," Garrett managed, but when he moved to slide off the counter, Drake gripped his ass and pulled him forward. Garrett wrapped his legs around Drake's waist to keep from falling and found himself lifted and on the move.

"This okay?" Drake asked as he reached the bedroom and laid Garrett on the bed.

"Fuck, yes," Garrett replied, breathless.

"That's the general idea." Drake wore a sexy grin and reached for the hem of Garrett's T-shirt.

They shed clothes quickly until they lay naked together on the cool sheets, blankets, and comforter pushed aside. Garrett loved exploring Drake's body, tonguing his sensitive nipples, and mouthing at the hollow of his throat.

Drake's hands moved over him in a mixture of confidence and reverence. Garrett knew Drake had more experience than he did, but the careful way Drake touched him, even when they were both very aroused, reassured Garrett that there was more than just lust between him.

"I have an idea, something to try that isn't exactly anal but gets us a step closer," Drake said. "Are you up for it?"

Garrett couldn't help snickering since his member was obviously, painfully up. "Talk fast before I die from blue balls."

"Ever done dry humping? Technically, it's intercrural sex, but that doesn't sound spicy enough."

"Thigh sex? I think I read something about monks in the Middle Ages claiming it didn't count."

"Whatever gets you off counts," Drake assured him. "It isn't the same as anal, and it's not going to hit your prostate, but there's a lot to be said for getting some full body feels."

"Okay," Garrett said. "I'm in."

They took their time removing clothing, doing plenty of

touching and kissing between layers. Garrett's previous encounters—he couldn't really call them lovers—had been about getting to the good stuff as fast as possible.

Drake's rock-hard cock assured Garrett that he wanted to get off. But he also took his time to make sure Garrett felt loved and wanted, to see his pleasure as a priority and not an afterthought. And, instead of being impatient with Garrett's inexperience, Drake looked for ways to pleasure them both without pressure, minding Garrett's boundaries.

Garrett never realized respect was so sexy.

"So—I was thinking, if this is okay with you, we could try it with you doing me," Drake said, with the lube in hand. "So we slick me up, thighs and ass crack, and you ride me. That way, you get some of the experience, and you know for sure no lines will get crossed."

Which is a very nice way to acknowledge that I've got trust issues after the last time I tried something like this. I want to keep this man forever. He gets me.

"Okay. What do I do?"

Drake gave him a rakish grin. "You fuck between my legs like you're riding a racehorse."

"But what about—"

"I promise you that I will get off," Drake assured him. "Just thinking about it has me revved. So let's give this a try."

They tossed the last pieces of clothing on the floor. Garrett watched, painfully hard, as Drake made a show of slicking his upper thighs and crack with plenty of lube and then wiping what remained on Garrett's very stiff prick.

"How—"

"Probably easiest from behind." Drake got onto his knees and elbows, presenting his very fine ass to be fucked. "Ride me, cowboy."

Garrett moved into position and ran his tongue down Drake's spine, pleased to get a shiver in return. He reached around and gave a few tugs on Drake's cock, keeping him hard.

"C'mon, Garrett. Fuck me like you mean it," Drake growled.

Garrett took Drake by the hips and slid between his thighs. Even with the slick, friction nearly undid him right away, and he caught his breath, freezing to keep from coming too fast. He slid forward and back again, setting up a rhythm.

"Yeah, just like that," Drake moaned.

Garrett leaned forward, blanketing Drake with his body. The heady smell of sweat, sex, and lube filled the air. Garrett licked, kissed, and sucked Drake's skin, loving the slide of his cock between strong thighs, appreciating the way Drake's muscular back rippled with the tension of holding them up.

"Oh, yeah," Drake said. "So good, Garrett. Keep it up. Want to feel you come. Want to feel you spill all over me."

Garrett let his cock slip between Drake's firm ass cheeks, recognizing the trust involved that he wouldn't suddenly change his mind and penetrate without warning or prep. *That's why he wanted me to do him first. Trust.*

Garrett felt such a mix of love and lust that he thought he would lose it right there, but he managed to keep going a while longer. He tried to reach around with one hand for Drake's cock, but Drake batted him away.

"I've got it covered. Get yourself off on my body, Garrett. Fuck me good."

Garrett felt his climax rise from deep inside, tightening his balls and making his cock painfully hard before he began to shoot, covering Drake's thighs, his ass, and the bedspread with his come.

Drake went rigid beneath him and cried out, trembling with the force of his orgasm. They collapsed together, tangled up in a slick, sticky mess and too blissed out to care.

He rolled to one side with a groan, and his oversensitive cock slipped from between Drake's legs. Drake brought his hand up to stroke the side of Garrett's face with his fingertips.

"Guess you enjoyed that?" he teased with a wicked gleam in his eyes.

"Looks like you did too."

"Feel good?"

"You have to ask?"

"Really good. Was it okay for you? I feel like I got all the fun."

"Oh, yeah."

For a few minutes, they were quiet, just touching and grounding themselves in each other.

"I get it. Why you wanted me to go first. The trust," Garrett murmured.

"I thought it would be easier to show you than tell you."

Garrett nuzzled close, and Drake wrapped an arm around him, drawing him near. "Thank you." He buried his face against Drake's chest. "For understanding."

Drake raised a hand to stroke Garrett's hair. "Of course. I care about you."

Garrett caught the stammer, the quick change of wording, and smiled, feeling warmth bloom in his chest. "I care about you too," he said, willing to dance around the L word but sure of it all the same.

"We should shower, or we'll be stuck together in the morning," Drake pointed out. "And the comforter is going to need laundered."

"Okay." Garrett pressed a kiss to Drake's shoulder and rolled away with a sigh. "Why don't you get the water at the right temperature, and I'll strip the top layer off the bed. I'll join you in a couple of minutes."

As Drake ran the shower, Garrett bundled up the soiled

comforter and shoved it into the closet with the dirty laundry basket.

He felt fluttery and excited like he hadn't felt since his teenage years but with a more grounded, sensual tether than in those early days. The romance novels talked about mate bonds, and Garrett wondered if Drake, as a psychic, had sensed Garrett's feelings even without words.

There's so much left to explore, so many ways to make each other feel good and loved. If I wasn't over the moon already, I am now.

I'll pretend we're still taking it slowly, for Drake's sake, but I'm all in. I hope he will be too.

CHAPTER SIX

DRAKE

*J*esus, Drake. That looks like a slaughterhouse," Clark said through Drake's headset.

"Smells like one too," he murmured.

"Bodies?"

"Not yet," Drake replied. "And if I find any, let's hope they stay dead."

Drake had gone to check the warehouses by the river. He heeded Garrett's warning about the danger, which was even greater because Drake was looking for trouble and hoping he found it.

"Any idea what went down?" Clark asked.

"Not yet. I'd bet the blood on the floor isn't all human, but we'd need the forensics folks to confirm that."

Drake had his gun in hand as he made his way through the shadowy, abandoned space. Light filtered down from dirty windows high overhead. Someone had attempted a cleanup. Other than the bloodstains on the concrete floor, not much had been left behind, just pieces of wooden pallets, glass shards, bits of scorched metal, and yellowed papers. The whole place smelled of mildew and rat piss.

It's not exactly like my vision, but close enough.

"Picking up on anything else?"

Drake concentrated, focusing on his psychic sense. "Magic. Fairly fresh, somewhat sloppy, and plenty of traces. I'm thinking that maybe some of McElvoy and Rankin's toughs fought it out," he added, referring to the two largest local supernatural crime families.

"That would explain the blood."

"I'm not seeing anything that looks like a lab or drug production equipment," Drake reported. "So if they made the stuff here, they cleaned that up well enough that it's not easily visible."

"Could have been a distribution site or just a drug drop. Or maybe a big, empty space to have a witchy gang war. He ran it through a bunch of shell companies and intermediaries, but the warehouse belonged to McElvoy, and before him, Fletcher Swain, that dark warlock you helped smack down," Clark said. "Their employment agency was in an office building in the same business park."

The employment agency was a cover for trafficking shifters and low-level witches who had enough power to be useful but not enough to free themselves.

Drake put on latex gloves and pulled out his test kit, swabbing spots on the floor, doors, and walls, then waiting for the quick analysis to turn color.

"Yeah, the tests are positive for paranormal pharmaceuticals," he told Clark.

"All right—you got what you came for. Don't hang around. Bad neighborhood—and you attract trouble."

"Roger that."

Something bugged Drake, but he couldn't quite figure out why. He walked back to where the floor was stained red and turned in a slow circle, taking in the scene. Then he realized what was missing. There were blood stains by each place where a body had fallen—but not large enough to indicate a fatal amount.

Something drained them or took them elsewhere to die.

He could make a case for either scenario and wondered if the witches had turned their vampire allies loose on the casualties before hauling the bodies away.

"Don't push your luck," Clark warned. "You got what you wanted. Get out of there."

Drake looked around the empty warehouse, frustrated. So far, he still wasn't entirely certain who posed the biggest threat since the dark witch, Fletcher Swain, had been destroyed. "Heading back," he said under his breath.

"Stay on the link until you're in the truck and away from there," Clark told him.

"Fine with me."

Drake remained hyper-alert until he was in his Silverado and pulling away from the business park.

Just as he pulled onto the main road, a dark figure suddenly appeared in front of him. Swearing loudly, he wrenched the wheel to the side to keep from hitting what appeared to be a man dressed in oversized, ragged clothing.

Drake braced for impact—and went right through the apparition.

"What the hell?"

The ghost loomed large in his rearview mirror. Drake felt a force shove the truck hard, making it swerve as he fought to keep control. The spirit flickered and vanished, only to appear in front of him once more in a spectral game of cat and mouse.

This time, headlights glared from the oncoming lane, narrowing his options for maneuvering. Drake ignored the instinct to jerk the wheel to avoid the figure and braced himself for impact as he drove right toward—and through—the phantom.

He gripped the steering wheel white-knuckled as his heart pounded. The car that passed him hadn't even slowed, making him wonder if the ghost was something only he could see—or a spirit sent as a warning to cause an accident.

Not for the first time, he wished he had some Batmobile-style alterations that would let him spray salted holy water from the grillwork.

Instead, he began to chant a banishment ritual, glad that the cab was warded and salted to avoid picking up ghostly hitchhikers. The spirit winked out, and Drake checked his mirrors to make sure it hadn't taken up residence in the bed of his truck. He didn't see anything, but just to be sure, he chanted a Latin exorcism since he wasn't certain what type of apparition had attacked him.

Was it related to the warehouse? One of the people who died there? Or is this just a bad luck stretch of road with a repeater ghost living out his last moments?

He kept an eye on his rearview mirror but didn't spot anyone following him. Once he was back at the hotel, he ran a scan to assure himself that no one had put a bug or a tracker on his vehicle and breathed a little easier to find none.

After he cleared his room for intrusions, Drake let out a long breath, poured himself a cup of cold coffee, and heated it in the microwave.

He set up his laptop on the table and opened the files Clark and Faye had sent him before accepting Clark's video meeting invitation.

"Glad you got back safely," Clark said. "I hate big, abandoned industrial buildings. Too many damn hiding places."

"Pretty sure that's why the bad guys seem to love them." Drake took a gulp of coffee, needing the caffeine jolt.

"It's taken a while, but I think I've unsnarled a few things," Clark said. "Fletcher Swain was the bigwig, and he'd had a century to amass his holdings and get rid of rivals. When you and your friends stopped him, it didn't just break up his fake wellness business—it sent all the underlings scrambling for pieces of the empire."

"Which we suspected."

"Yeah, but we didn't know who grabbed what. Now I think I've got a better idea."

"Fill me in." Drake hoped the coffee hit his system soon. He needed that jolt.

"Doane McGill is the local top honcho vampire," Clark told him. "He worked with Swain and Osborn, and he also seems to have done business with the two main supernatural syndicate families. That's impressive, because the McElvoy family and the Rankin family have been at odds since their ancestors stepped off the boat from Ireland. Maybe before then."

"That's probably true," Drake agreed. "Let me guess—the two crime families are fighting over who gets to take over the spoils from the witches, though Osborn's operation was the plum. The McElvoys seem to have claimed the pharmaceuticals and the Rankins have the trafficking."

"McGill supplies people with supernatural abilities to Rankin, who farms them out to the highest bidder," Clark continued. "And McGill also has contacts who ensure that the drugs are optimized for supernatural metabolisms, and he finds dealers and distributors that won't skim off the profits or use the product."

"Playing both ends against the middle?"

"That seems to be the case. No matter who loses, he wins," Clark replied.

"Do we have any intel on McGill?" Drake felt like they were chasing their tails, going around in circles while something essential stayed out of reach.

"Doane McGill was born to a well-to-do family and was turned by a vampire in 1900 when he was twenty-five years old," Clark said. "He built on that family wealth with success in several industries, but he seems to have a fondness for chemistry, so he's been a big supporter of the drug business, and he has connections everywhere that help him stay under the radar."

"And he's got his fingers in the trafficking pie?"

"Yep. Then again, vampires are good at glamouring people—plus the zombie drugs make that easier. If he has his brood working with him, that could make securing the victims much simpler," Clark added. "I'm sure the roofies that lower the ability to fight compulsion play a big role in the shifter trafficking trade."

"Great info," Drake said. "Now we've just got to figure out the best way to take their operation down."

"Both the McElvoy and Rankin families have their own witches. And we know that Swain and Osborn eliminated any witches they thought were strong enough to challenge them. That's not as reassuring as it might sound because the *stregas* could still be fairly powerful but not have posed a threat," Clark cautioned.

"If the families have been at odds for so long, I'm surprised they're dividing the spoils," Drake mused.

"Yeah, me too. It might be that they don't think they're strong enough to fight to keep everything and win," Clark replied. "If they split things up now, maybe they figure they can come back and take it all later when they're strong enough to crush the competition."

"I hate witch wars," Drake muttered.

"And that brings me to the other piece. Jennings Weston is a witch who wants to be the heir to Fletcher Swain. He's bided his time and has managed to avoid swearing fealty to either of the syndicate families while playing up to the vampires. Swain apparently didn't see him as a threat, and I think Weston engineered that. Colletta's witch is one of Weston's disciples."

"But Swain is gone." Drake pieced it together as he spoke. "Does Weston think he can fill Swain's shoes?"

"Maybe he doesn't have to," Clark said. "If he carves out a piece for himself, he can let everyone else do what they want with Osborn's drug business. As for taking over for Swain, if Jennings and McGill revive Swain's spiritual retreat business, they can get their food to deliver itself to them—and have all the blood and juicy emotions they need to feed themselves."

"Fuck. I hate those types. They're almost always a scam, even when they aren't literally sucking people dry," Drake muttered.

"I'm right there with you," Clark agreed.

"So we've got a gang war over territory and zombie drugs plus vampires—and a witch who might be more powerful than he lets on," Drake summarized. "You know that saying about cutting off the snake's head and having a hydra pop up in its place? I feel like that's what we've got with Swain out of the picture."

"If you expect law enforcement to ever catch all the criminals, you're going to be very disappointed," Clark said. "It's more like Whack-a-Mole. Swain did a lot of damage for a very long time. I don't think that anyone thought taking him out would rid West Virginia of evil. But it's the best we can do—knock off the worst ones and keep an eye out for the next crop."

"Right now, what we've got are suspicions, and we need something solid to act on." He got up and started to pace the room. "A lab location. A group of trafficked shifters being moved. A big drug delivery. Even if we could bust them on something smaller, it wouldn't be enough to shut them down, but it would be a start."

"Be patient. Something will turn up," Clark replied. "That's the hardest lesson I learned in law enforcement and the most valuable."

"Always at the wrong time and in the worst possible way," Drake agreed. "Every time."

CHAPTER SEVEN

GARRETT

*W*ell, that was an afternoon to remember—for all the wrong reasons," Garrett said as he stripped off his latex gloves and dropped them into the garbage.

"We're not closed yet." Kirsten sprayed cleaner on the stainless steel examining table and wiped it down with paper towels before removing and discarding her gloves. "Don't tempt fate."

"Is there a full moon? I swear that must be it." Garrett pushed his hair back and rolled his head to loosen a stiff neck.

"Could be. But the last time I checked, we still had a full waiting room."

Garrett sighed. "I keep telling myself that busy beats the alternatives, but I don't always believe it."

"Maybe everyone decided to get their pets in to be seen before the weekend. Or there's a virus going around," Kirsten suggested.

"Yeah." Garrett wished he had a triple latte. He rubbed his eyes. "Okay. I'll head over to room three after I check on whether those two Parvo vaccination dogs had a reaction. See you there."

They had been swamped with sick and injured animals almost from the time the clinic doors opened. Some were serious and others less so, but Garrett did his best not to turn anyone away and so he had muddled through a caseload that was half again as many patients as he would usually have seen.

Garrett knew that they could have sent some of the patients to the urgent care vet and the veterinary emergency room. But he didn't think they were sick enough to need that level of care, and he knew the expense to the owner would be more. Plus, these were regular patients, and Garrett didn't want to let them down.

So many people are already watching their pennies—I don't want to saddle them with a big bill if I can help it.

The rest of the afternoon passed in a blur. Given the backlog, Garrett didn't get to chat as much as he would have liked with the owners, something that made his day more social and tended to decrease their stress. On the other hand, thanks to his staff pitching in to help, he worked his way through the queue of patients before closing time.

"Almost done." Kirsten peeked out toward the waiting room. "And it's nearly time to quit for the day. Good job!"

Mrs. McHenry's nauseated boxer and Mr. Sanders's constipated orange cat were the last two patients and their appointments were uncomplicated. Garrett took a swig of his energy drink and leaned against the counter, closing his eyes for just a minute.

He'd just wrapped up with Mr. Sanders's cat when his watch buzzed, telling him that it was five o'clock.

"Hey—I know you said you had some paperwork," Kirsten said. "Do you want me to take Bailey to the dog park with Cuddles, and you can pick him up on the way home?"

"You're a godsend, and this is why you're one of Bailey's favorite people," Garrett told her gratefully. "I won't be here long, but Bailey paces when he's ready to go, and it drives me nuts."

"Cuddles adores Bailey, and they both love the dog park," Kirsten said.

"Thank you. I'm not planning on being more than an hour if that. I really appreciate it."

"It's definitely not a hardship. Plus they'll play harder with a buddy, and that means they'll sleep better when they get home," she said with a conspiratorial grin. Cuddles, her boxer-pittie mix, was a total pushover and loved Bailey like a brother from another mother.

He said goodnight to the staff and let the after hours cleaning crew in, then locked the door behind them and went to his office. The cleaners had their own key to lock up afterward. Having them in the building kept it from being too quiet. Tonight, they finished up more quickly than usual, leaving him alone again.

Garrett tried not to let paperwork build up, but he had left earlier than usual the last few nights when he had plans with Drake, so he had a small stack of forms and files to wade through. Without Bailey prodding him to go home, he expected to breeze through the documents and be on his way quickly.

He frowned when he heard a strange noise from the waiting room, but it wasn't repeated so he went back to his papers. Garrett had a sudden spike of fear and pain that he knew didn't belong to him. He reeled, wondering if one of the dogs boarding with them had an unexpected illness, and when he looked up, found himself staring at the business end of a Glock.

"No quick moves," Colletta said. "Brian's been hurt, and I need you to save him."

Garrett's eyes widened. "I'm not set up as an emergency room."

"You do surgery, right? You know how."

Garrett nodded. "Basic sorts. Not the specialized kind. I really don't think—"

"Brian got stabbed in the shoulder. He's in pain, and I want you to fix him up."

"Stabbed? You mean—"

"I mean some bastard stabbed my dog, and I want you to make sure Brian is okay," Colletta snapped.

Garrett raised both hands, palms out, in surrender. "Okay. Where is he?"

"I carried him into your OR. Please—help him."

Colletta was a mobster and probably worse, but Brian was an innocent, and Garrett couldn't say no to a hurt dog even without a gun pointed at him.

"Show me," he told Colletta. "And quit pointing that thing at me."

Colletta walked behind him to the operating room. Brian lay wrapped in a bloody blanket on the floor. He raised his head to look at Garrett with sad eyes.

Garrett hunkered down beside him. "Did you get hurt, baby boy?"

"Don't worry—I took care of the one who did it," Colletta said in a voice that sent a shiver down Garett's back.

Garrett tried to think of a way out of the situation that didn't end with him dead. He came up blank. He was unlikely to get a chance to call Drake or the police, and he certainly didn't want to involve his staff. As long as Colletta needed him, Garrett figured he would be relatively safe.

And Brian couldn't help belonging to a criminal.

"I need to lay out supplies and scrub up for surgery," Garrett told Colletta, mustering his nerve. Here in the operating room, he was the expert, and a gun didn't change that.

"Most of the supplies are in those cabinets. I won't know until I examine Brian whether or not he needs blood. If he does, that's in the refrigerator in the back. You can follow me around as I get what I need, but if you want me to operate on your dog, I've got to have supplies."

"Be quick about it."

Garrett gritted his teeth but didn't want to provoke the man with the gun. *It's not Brian's fault his dad is a jerk.*

He found most of the things he needed in the operating room cabinets but motioned for Colletta to follow him when he went to get the medications required for surgery from the locked refrigerator in the back.

"This is the pain medication and anesthesia," he told Colletta. "When I'm done, I'll get some pills for him to keep him comfortable after you leave."

Assuming he lets me live and they don't find my body in the morning.

His phone was in his pocket, turned to silent, but he didn't dare try to text Drake or summon help.

Garrett and Colletta lifted Brian on a blanket onto the operating table and shimmied him onto the stainless steel surface. Brian whimpered but looked at Garrett with big, trusting eyes.

"Fix him," Colletta ordered.

"I do better when I'm not nervous, and having a gun pointed at me isn't going to help me relax," Garrett said. "Ease up and let me do my job."

"So do it. I'm waiting."

Garrett drew in a deep breath and let it out, trying to focus on helping Brian and not on the gun pointed his direction. He didn't have a date with Drake tonight, so no one would notice anything was amiss until he didn't go to pick up Bailey from Kirsten. By that time, it might be too late.

Focus on the patient. Brian deserves care.

Colletta fretted in the corner, gun still in hand, while Garrett prepped Brian and gave him anesthesia. He was a little surprised it took more than usual but felt relieved when the dog gradually relaxed into a deep sleep.

Only then could Garrett fully focus on the wound to Brian's shoulder. "How did this happen?"

"None of your business."

Garrett turned to face Colletta and met his gaze. "You want me to fix this? I need to know what I'm dealing with. It looks like a knife wound. What happened?"

Colletta gave him a deadly glare. "There was a fight. Doesn't matter what about—but someone came at me, and Brian tried to protect me. He got the knife that was meant for me. I fixed the problem—won't happen again." His smirk suggested he had implemented a very final solution.

Garrett's stomach twisted. When he had met Colletta, he thought the man gave off gangster vibes, but he didn't think the man was an actual mobster. Now, Garrett wasn't so sure.

"Okay, that helps. A sharp blade is better than a rusted piece of farm equipment. Less chance of infection, cleaner edges."

Colletta grunted in acknowledgment as Garrett continued to narrate what he was doing. "I'm going to flush the wound to ensure it's as clean as possible and stitch it closed. Then I'll put an antibiotic cream on the surface and wrap it. I'll give you antibiotic pills for him so he doesn't get an infection, as well as pain pills so he'll be comfortable. He shouldn't do much moving for several days, nothing strenuous for at least a week."

Colletta stood against the far wall with his hands clasped in front of him and his gun still in his grip. He watched Garrett's every movement. If the man wasn't holding him hostage, Garrett might have appreciated how much a tough guy could care for his dog. Now, he just felt bad that Brian had a criminal for a father.

Garrett pushed all that from his mind and focused on his patient. The wound missed anything vital and probably wouldn't cause permanent damage. Brian needed a blood transfusion, and he would be sore for a while, but with rest and medicine, he would recover nicely, maybe even without a limp.

He managed to keep himself together until he tied off the last stitch. Until then, his hands didn't shake, but they were trembling as he set the scissors aside.

"Well?" Colletta asked.

"He's going to be okay—*if* he gets rest, stays off his feet as much as possible for a week, no strenuous activity, and he'll need medicine for pain and to prevent infection," Garrett told him.

"That's good. You did good, Doc."

Garrett relaxed a little since it didn't seem like he was going to get shot in the next few minutes.

"What stuff will he need for recovery? Pack him a bag." Colletta gestured with the gun.

"Pain pills, antibiotic pills, antibiotic ointment for the site, gauze bandages, surgical tape, and the dreaded cone to keep him from licking the stitches," Garrett listed off. "I'm giving him blood, so he shouldn't need another transfusion. The pain pills should make him groggy so he doesn't try to be too active."

"Put it together."

Garrett figured the longer he could keep Colletta happy, the more likely he was to get out of this alive. He gathered everything and put it in a bag.

"You're pretty good at stitching up, Doc."

"Got a lot of practice in vet school."

"Pack what you'll need for a couple of days. You're coming with us to take care of Brian."

Garrett's blood ran cold. "I…that's not…I can't—"

The gun rose to point at his chest. "That was an order, not a request. Don't worry—I'll pay you very well. But I'm going to be busy, and Brian needs someone looking out for him. So you come with me, keep an eye on him, and in a couple of days, I bring you back. Easy peasy."

Except for the part where I don't get a choice. And how you'll figure that I know too much afterward and you can't let me go after all.

Rushing the guy with the gun would be suicidal, and Colletta probably had thirty pounds of muscle on him, even if Garrett was taller. Colletta had the look of a brawler, so he probably didn't even need the gun to knock Garrett out, toss him over his shoulder, and throw him into a panel truck.

I'm going to disappear, and no one will know what happened.

"Okay." Garrett figured it was a good idea to appease the guy with the gun. "I need to get my go-bag from my office. I keep one packed for emergencies. And I have to gather the medicine Brian needs."

"Hurry—and don't try anything stupid."

Garrett tried to take deep breaths to calm his nerves and still his shaking hands. He moved slowly, buying himself time to think. If anyone had noticed Colletta picking the lock and reported it, police would have arrived by now. Garrett hadn't set the alarm because he was still in the building. He and Drake had both planned to work late so no one except Kirsten and Bailey would notice he didn't come home.

Since Colletta didn't seem inclined to let him clean up the operatory, Garrett's staff would probably figure out what happened, and Colletta was the likely suspect. But the regular police wouldn't know how to follow the clues, and no one was likely to think about calling Drake. Eventually,

Drake would come looking for him, but the trail would be cold by then.

Colletta stood in the doorway as Garrett bustled around his office. He knew he wouldn't get away with writing a note, but he stuck one hand in his pocket as he angled away from Colletta, and hoped that he could send a text to Drake.

Garrett: *Kidnapped. Car*

"What the fuck do you think you're doing?" Colletta snatched the phone away and smashed it to the floor.

"I—"

"No more stalling. Grab what you have and Brian's medicine. I need you to get him into my SUV."

Garrett knew from the look in Colletta's eyes that he had pushed his luck as far as it would stretch. While the mobster wanted Garrett to care for Brian, he might decide the vet knew too much and make a clean break.

"Okay. I'm ready."

They got Brian into the back, and the sedatives kept the dog from minding being jostled.

Colletta dangled a pair of handcuffs. "Put these on."

Garrett complied. "These go on your ankles. No funny stuff."

Garrett snapped the cuffs closed with a sinking heart. His chances of escape were nil, and his likelihood of surviving this adventure were looking worse by the moment.

Colletta smacked him in the temple with his gun, and everything went black.

GARRETT WOKE with a rag stuffed in his mouth. He was still bound hand and foot, and the SUV had stopped.

He heard raised voices, Colletta arguing with someone outside the SUV.

"You brought a doctor here for your damn dog?" a stranger demanded.

"If he can stitch up a dog, he can sew up a person," Colletta countered. "You've got the drugs, but no one who knows how to do doctoring."

"And you think he's just going to go along with it?"

"For as long as we need him." Colletta's tone sent a chill down Garrett's spine. *Once I'm not useful and Brian is out of the woods, I'm toast.*

Two other toughs came to carry Brian, surprisingly gentle. They lifted Garrett from the car and set him on his feet. "Be careful with him." Colletta gestured with his gun. He turned to Garrett. "What are you staring at? Follow them. Where the dog goes, you go."

Garrett looked down at his feet. Colletta grumbled but unlocked the cuffs on his ankles, although his wrists were still bound.

Garrett fell in behind the men, heading into the basement of a shuttered industrial building that looked like it had been out of business for a long time. He had no idea where he was or how long it had taken them to get there since he had been unconscious. Right now, his head throbbed, and he thought about taking one of the pain pills he had brought for the dog.

They went into a windowless room with a steel door. Inside were two cots, two blankets, and two very questionable pillows. Buckets in the corner were probably meant to be toilets. A few bottles of water stood near the door, along with a filled water bowl for Brian.

The toughs put Brian on one of the cots, threw Garrett's bags onto the other cot, and left.

Garrett looked at Colletta. "So how does this work?"

Colletta shrugged. "Fix my dog, you don't die."

"It's going to take a few days to get him feeling better—not one hundred percent, but better. He'll need food and water, and so will I to be able to take care of him." He figured he might as well put his most basic needs up front. "And when he's in better shape, your people will take me back to the clinic?"

Colletta gave him a smile that made Garrett's blood freeze. "Yeah. We'll take you back."

I'm going to die here. As soon as I'm not useful for Brian, and maybe for treating some of their soldiers, they're going to kill me.

No one will know where to find the body.

I won't get to say goodbye to Drake.

Bailey will never understand why I didn't come home.

Colletta unlocked the handcuffs then locked the door behind him, leaving Garrett and Brian alone. Garrett walked the perimeter of the small room, looking for cameras or microphones. He didn't see any but doubted anyone thought he would be telling a dog the secrets of the universe.

Without his phone, he couldn't contact Drake. Garrett moved his bed closer to where Brian lay and sat down.

"Guess it's just you and me." He gently petted the dog's side. Brian snuffled and shimmied, still asleep.

"You seem like a very nice dog. How did you get mixed up in all this?" If Garrett held any hope that being a devoted pet owner meant Colletta was not also a cold-blooded killer that had fizzled.

"I'm glad he takes good care of you," Garrett went on since he had nothing else to do. Even though Brian was still out cold from the pills, gentle contact and a soothing voice would help reduce anxiety and let him relax. At least he could do some good during what were likely to be his last hours on Earth.

"I had a black Lab when I was a kid," Garrett continued.

"She lived to be fifteen. Dora. Great dog. You'd have liked her. Best fetcher ever. Well, until Bailey. You met Bailey when you came to the office before. I bet you two would have gotten along great."

He told Brian stories about his childhood dogs and walks he had taken with Bailey. After that, he thought of the funny things that had happened at the clinic and recounted the plot of the last two series he had binged.

"I'm not much of a singer, or I'd sing you to sleep." Garrett walked over and took a bottle of water to soothe his throat. It looked unopened, and he figured that poisoning him after they just brought him to help with the dog didn't make any sense, so he took a chance and drank it down.

Garrett stroked Brian's side, taking as much comfort from the contact as he was giving. He thought about Drake and how he had hoped their budding relationship would go.

I figured that we'd still date after his case wrapped up. Wheeling isn't very far away. Then, when the time was right, we'd move in together, maybe somewhere in the middle between his office and the clinic.

Down the line, after a while, maybe we'd get married. Bailey would have been a cute ring bearer. We'd figure out how to make our schedules work, go on vacations, and get old. We'd bitch about things and make up.

I want that life, that future. And the way things are going, I don't think it's going to happen.

At least it's early in our time together. We've both fallen hard, but we haven't been together very long. Maybe that will make it easier for Drake. I never meant to hurt him.

He probably can't adopt Bailey, given his schedule. I hope Kirsten or someone from our office gives him a good home.

They'll need to sell the clinic. If someone takes it over, maybe they'll keep the employees—we have a good team. I'd just gotten everything up and running the way I'd always wanted it. I thought I'd have decades to keep building.

Guess there's no way of knowing how long you've got.

If I ever get out of here, I'm posting a strict "No Mobsters" policy. Except that wouldn't be fair to their dogs, who didn't do anything wrong. Brian is a sweetie. Not his fault Colletta is a scumbag.

Over the next few hours, Garrett talked and sang to Brian and made sure he took his medicine. The pain pills made Brian groggy, so he drifted in and out of sleep.

Later in the day, the door opened. One of the mobsters came in with a bowl of food for Brian and a sandwich for Garrett.

"Eat. Boss is going to need you to help him with something later on."

Garrett tried to ignore the ominous comment and did his best to get Brian to eat and drink before turning to his food. The ham and cheese sandwich wasn't bad, but given the stress, Garrett didn't taste it.

Garrett put aside his empty plate and took a swig of water from his bottle. *What's going on out there? Something brought Drake to Moundsville, and whatever it was had to be pretty big to involve the feds.*

He had heard rumors that other vets had run into animals dosed with unusual painkillers and anxiety medications, ones that weren't standard pharmacy issue.

What if they weren't really pets? I think I'd notice if I ended up with a shifter because of the way I can pick up on animals' thoughts, but would a regular vet with no psychic ability notice?

How many shifters and weres are out there, passing for pets when they need medical help because they are more likely to get caught by regular doctors than by veterinarians?

Brian was still heavily sedated, so Garrett pulled his cot

next to the dog's and decided to catch some sleep while he could.

They're probably going to kill me one way or another, so if they do it in my sleep, at least I won't see them coming. He stretched out one arm so that he could stay in contact with Brian, soothing the dog and taking comfort from his company.

"Hey, wake up."

Garrett felt something hard poke him in the ribs and woke to find himself staring down a shotgun. Colletta stood in the doorway with his handgun while a tough kept the shotgun pointed at Garrett.

"A couple of the boys got hurt. They need stitched up. You're a doc. I need you to take care of them."

Garrett gave Brian a pat, unsure whether he would see the dog again, then he followed Colletta with the tough guy behind them.

What he saw told him that his guess about being in the basement of an abandoned industrial building was correct. They wound through a maze of windowless concrete walls until Colletta stopped in front of a door.

"Here we go, Doc. I'm counting on you to do your thing and take care of my boys. Do a good job, and everything will work out peachy for you."

Garrett didn't believe a word of it, but he tried to keep his skepticism from showing in his eyes. The door swung open, and he saw half a dozen young men milling about in what looked to be a makeshift medical station.

"Gunshot wounds, some knife wounds, and a couple of broken bones," Colletta told him. "You tell Freddie here what you need, and he'll go get it. I'm going to hang out and make sure my boys don't give you a hard time." He gave Garrett a hard stare. "You'd have to be a smart man to get through medical school, so I'm counting on you not to try anything dumb. Understand?"

Garrett nodded, momentarily defeated. "I want to triage them—see the injuries—and then I'll know what I need. For starters, rubbing alcohol, clean cloths, sutures, suturing needles, antibiotic cream. I won't know what more until I've had a look."

Colletta nodded and motioned for one of his toughs to follow Garrett from patient to patient and take notes. "He says he needs something, you write it down. Got it?" The man nodded, and Colletta went to stand by the door.

"They said you're a dog doctor. Is that true?" the first man asked as Garrett looked closely at the gunshot wound in his bicep.

"Does it matter? I'm the *only* doctor right now."

"Guess not. You'd better not snip my balls by accident or there'll be a world of hurt." His joke fell flat, and Garrett, overwhelmed by the situation, just stared at him in return.

"Did you get shot in the balls?"

"No," the mobster said.

"Then trust me, I'm not going near them."

Garrett dictated the needed supplies to the man who followed him around as Colletta watched from a distance.

"Think it'll fix right, Doc?" One of the men, barely out of his teens, gritted his teeth against the pain of a broken arm.

"I'd feel better about saying yes if we were in a real hospital," Garrett replied without looking up as he carefully palpated the arm, using as gentle a touch as he could and seeing the young man wince from the pain. "Pretty sure it's broken, but I can't tell more without an X-ray. I'll do my best, but even if the bone heals the way it should, you'll need some kind of physical therapy after the cast comes off."

"Just have him jerk off with that hand. He'll get plenty of exercise," one of the other men said, getting laughs and catcalls in response.

"Better than nothing." Garrett refused to be flustered.

After he had made one round, his assistant went for supplies. Garrett wasn't sure where he found the items, but the man returned faster than expected.

"I need to wash up before I start and between patients," Garrett told his helper. "Since I don't see a sink in here, I need soap, a basin of water, and a clean towel. The water needs to be changed between each patient. You don't want your boys knocked out by an infection."

Garrett had to wait for the supplies, but he found reasons to dawdle so he could listen to what the injured men were saying.

"—fucking feds. Came outta nowhere."

"—gotta be a mole, and when we find him, he's gonna regret it."

"—bastards had good witches. We didn't have a chance."

Garrett's heart soared, thinking that Drake and his people had been behind the raid that laid up the mobsters. He might not get out of this in one piece, but it sounded like the Syndicate's days were numbered.

I guess I'll have to settle for being avenged if I don't end up being rescued.

He worked into the evening suturing and splinting, checking for infection, and doing his best to put his human patients at ease. For all that they might be stone-cold killers, they seemed oddly vulnerable despite their tough-guy posturing. Most were still in their mid-twenties, and Garrett wondered what the Syndicate had offered that persuaded them to join. He ran out of supplies, and the flunkies went to get more. While he waited, Garrett walked over to Colletta.

"How many of them are shifters?" He tested a theory that had occurred to him.

"What do you know about shifters?"

"Enough," Garrett replied, although his knowledge came from TV shows and movies, not clinical experience. "Are they? Because it's going to affect how I treat them."

If the shows were right, shifters had faster metabolisms than regular humans. That usually meant that they healed faster unless silver weapons were involved. Still, a doctor's help avoided bones setting badly, and even a fast metabolism needed help with gunshot wounds and the like.

"All of them," Colletta said after a pause.

"What sort of animal do they shift into? That might affect the dose of the painkiller."

"These are all wolves or big dogs like German Shepherds and Belgian Malinois," Colletta answered. "If that tells you anything."

Garrett nodded. "Actually, yes. Full-grown, their weights aren't far off from an adult human. That helps with dosages." He frowned. "You have special drugs for them? According to the TV shows, shifters have a higher-than-usual metabolism. Is that true?"

Colletta guffawed. "The TV shows? TV shows don't know shit about most things."

"Well excuse me, but we didn't cover shifters in vet school," Garrett shot back, made bold by his acceptance that he wasn't getting out of here.

Colletta gave him a look. "Guess not. So here's the deal— yes, the metabolism is faster. They burn off meds quicker than humans, and they need a higher dose for their size to feel it. Some human meds don't do a damn thing. There aren't any official medicines for their kind, so we made our own. The feds aren't too happy about that."

Bingo. That must be the case Drake's on, cracking down on illegal shifter drugs. Shit. I've landed right in the middle of things.

"How come no one makes shifter drugs on the down-low

—legally?" Garrett asked. "There are niche markets for everything."

Colletta looked at him as if he were stupid. "Because of the fuckin' FDA. Legit drugs have to get approvals. Can't get approval for shifter and vamp drugs without admitting there are shifters and vampires. Then the Area 51 guys come out with their white vans and shock collars and cart everyone away for experiments."

Garrett could follow the logic, even though he disapproved of the tactics. *Thanks for telling me that vampires are real. I didn't need to know that.*

"And it ain't just the FDA," Colletta went on. "There would be too many questions about who the drugs were for since their metabolisms are completely whack compared to humans. Once word gets out that they're real, the panic starts, the government gets involved, people decide to play monster hunter, and it all gets ugly."

Colletta shook his head. "Better to keep the feds out of it. We don't need them on our ass."

Meaning any kind of supervision would make it clear real fast who had teams of shifter hitmen.

"Do you have any of these wonder drugs here for me to use with them? And if you do, what kind? I need to know what I'm dealing with." Garrett's fatalism made him bold. Colletta seemed to respect his expertise—for now.

"We've got antibiotics that wipe out infections normies don't get. Pain killers strong enough to stop the pain and not wear off right away. Some drugs for things that regular people don't get but shifters and weres do, like a version of that Parvo thing."

Shifters can get Parvo? Garrett started thinking about what other diseases people usually thought of being strictly for animals and how mundane medicine would deal with the idea that shifters could be infected.

Wait, what? Weres? Like werewolves? My God, they're real too.

"Feel like you just fell through the looking glass?" Colletta chuckled. "Surprise. It's all true."

And now he has even less reason to let me go because I know too much. Maybe that's why he doesn't mind answering questions. I'm never going to have a chance to tell anyone.

Is this Drake's world—busting vampires and werewolves and the monster mafia? Could I have ever fit into that life if this hadn't happened?

Colletta's henchmen returned with the new supplies and a fresh bowl of hot water with soap. Garrett returned his attention to treating his patients.

On the plus side, no one bites—at least, I don't think they do. Then again, they've got nothing to prove to me since I'll be dead soon.

"The drugs your people make—are they addictive?" he asked Colletta as he cleaned up when he finished with the patient he'd been stitching. "Or do shifters burn them off too quick?"

Colletta shrugged. "People who want to find a place to hide will find it. If the drugs wear off, there are always more."

Not much of an answer, but it might not be a problem—or the mobsters are likely to die young before bad habits have a chance to catch up with them.

"What about recreational drugs? Werewolf weed? Vampire vapes? Monster meth?"

Colletta snorted. "That's good—you ought to be one of those marketing guys. Yeah, all that. Why not? Equal rights and all that jazz."

Garrett didn't want to know what a bad trip looked like for creatures who were stronger, faster, and had more teeth than humans.

"I gave them enough of the drugs to dull the pain and get them through the night," he reported to Colletta. "Same thing as with Brian—they'll heal better if you don't send them back into the fight too fast. Even with a faster metabolism, they won't heal overnight, and if they get re-injured, it will take even longer the next time even if they heal right."

When Garrett thought of his patients as mobsters, he feared them. When he pictured them as hurt dogs, he found the compassion to do his job in the right frame of mind. He didn't want any creature to be in pain or to not get appropriate care.

Just like the tiger. He had read about a zoo vet who had bonded with one of the tigers after he nursed it through a long illness. The tiger never tried to hurt him, not even a nip, while he was sick. The vet had told everyone it proved that tigers were just misunderstood. Except when the tiger recovered, it mauled and ate him.

At least getting shot is faster than being eaten. I guess there's a silver lining for everything.

Garrett had no idea of time in the windowless room. A runner brought in a pot of coffee and a mug for him to swig between patients. It only helped so much. He guessed that he had been up most of the night seeing to the injured men, but he wanted to make sure no one suffered complications before he could feel the job was done.

If they're going to kill me, at least it won't be for incompetence.

Once again, his thoughts drifted to Drake. If his team had been behind the fight that injured the shifters, did he know Garrett had been kidnapped? Would Drake have any way to link Colletta to the other targets of the night's battle and figure out what happened to Garrett?

He might not get here in time to save me, but at least he wouldn't think I ran off. Give me a decent burial—if they don't feed me to the wolves, that is.

Garrett felt totally spent when he finished. He saw first-hand how the illicit shifter drugs affected his patients and had to admit that for their heightened metabolisms, the medicines appeared to work very well.

A runner came in as he dozed in a chair waiting to make another round of checks on his patients. Garrett roused enough to see the stranger speak quietly to Colletta in an urgent, low tone.

"Hey, Doc. Gino is going to take you back to Brian. He's waking up, and you'd better go see how he's doing."

Garrett nodded wearily. After everything that day, he wanted nothing more than a few hours' sleep, but he knew that being useful kept him alive—at least for a while longer.

"Call me if anyone here runs a fever, gets sharp pain, or has any unusual symptoms," he told Colletta. "Those will be drug reactions, nothing to do with my stitching, but if they whack out and pop my sutures, it'll cause problems."

"Yeah, yeah. I'll let you know if that happens. Go fix my dog," Colletta growled.

Garrett followed the runner back to the room he shared with Brian. "Look, I'm dead on my feet," he told the man. "Can you bring me food? I don't care what kind. I'm no good if I pass out from hunger."

To his surprise, the man agreed. He locked Garrett in the room and stayed outside, presumably to fetch his requests.

Garrett approached Brian carefully, not wanting to scare the dog if he was half-asleep.

"You doing okay?"

Brian whined and looked at Garrett with sad eyes. It had been long enough that Garrett could dose him again with painkillers, but first, he offered food and water, which had their own healing properties.

"So do you stay a very pretty fellow, or change into a person?" Garrett asked the dog as he ate. He scratched Brian's ears and when the dog finished eating, led him to where their jailers had put down a pad for him to use for a bathroom.

"Sorry, dude. This is what we've got. You should see what they gave me," Garrett said when Brian looked up at him, confused.

Once Brian finished his business and drank some water, Garrett gave him another dose of pain medicine that would help him sleep.

"You're a very good boy," Garrett told Brian as he curled up on the cot with his blanket. "Very brave. I'm sorry you got hurt. Maybe you can get your master to change jobs to something where people don't shoot each other."

If Brian was really a shifter, then he was likely all-in on the Mob like Colletta. It made Garrett sad that he probably wouldn't like person Brian nearly as much as dog Brian.

Garrett dozed next to Brian until he heard the door open. He went from sleepy to wide awake, wondering whether they had more wounded to treat or had decided to get rid of him.

Colletta walked in with a man Garrett didn't recognize but whose presence made his hindbrain want to run and hide. The man was taller than Colletta and slender, with fine, almost aristocratic features. He had dark hair and very pale skin, and while he was just dressed in a black shirt and jeans, he moved with predatory grace.

Colletta turned back to the door and ushered in a second stranger who had a strange glint in his eyes.

"You've been helpful, so we need to keep you with us a while longer," Colletta said. "And there are...situations going on outside that will require my attention. We can't have you running off. So I've asked Paul here to make sure that doesn't happen."

Garrett backed up, not sure what was going on, but positive he wouldn't like it. "I said I wouldn't run away."

"Of course you did. And of course, you were lying," Colletta said easily, as if they weren't talking about Garrett's life. "Which would be unfortunate. So my associate is going to make sure you won't leave without permission."

The slender stranger moved so quickly that Garrett didn't see the motion until the man had crossed the room and grabbed him by the collar from behind.

"Wait! What—"

He felt two needle-sharp punctures in the side of his neck and gasped in pain and fear.

Vampires are real. Is he a vampire? Oh God, is he going to turn me?

In just seconds, the man stepped back, releasing Garrett. Two rivulets of warm blood trickled down Garrett's neck. The other man Garrett didn't recognize spoke strange-sounding words that sent a shiver of energy through his body and left him gasping.

Colletta looked amused. Garrett wanted to be angry but found he couldn't muster the energy.

"Until I release you, we are bound blood to blood. You will only leave if I permit it or if you die. If you leave without my permission, you will die within three days," Paul said.

"Confused? Let me explain. Paul is, indeed, a vampire. He's fed from you, which creates a bond. He hasn't done anything to turn you; at least, not yet," Colletta added with a smirk.

"The bite creates a link between you and him, and the link, along with the witch's spell, forges a compulsion. You can't harm him, and if he forbids it, you can't harm me or anyone else, either. But look at the bright side—you won't need those handcuffs anymore," Colletta said.

Garrett wanted to be furious. He knew he should be terrified. All he could manage was a remarkable level of unconcern.

"You've been very useful. I'm grateful for what you've done for Brian. Maybe we'll keep you around. Having a doc comes in handy."

With that, Colletta, the witch, and the vampire left. They turned their backs on Garrett and did not hurry, knowing he was powerless to attack or escape.

Garrett stared at the door for a moment, then sank to the floor, distraught. *I'm screwed. I can't even run away. If Drake finds me and tries to rescue me, would I fight back? When they're done with me, will they kill me or turn me?*

Normally, he would have taken comfort hugging the dog, but not knowing if Brian was really a shifter made it weird. Garrett curled up in a ball with his arms around his knees and tried to calm down.

Are they lying about not turning me? If Drake found me, would he see me as one of the monsters he hunts?

Vampires are immortal. I bet the compulsion means I can't harm myself.

I am truly fucked, and definitely not in a good way.

To his surprise, Brian staggered over and lay down beside him. He nudged Garrett's hand and pressed against his side.

"You shouldn't have moved," Garrett said quietly, although the sentimental gesture affected him.

Brian gave a soft whine and shimmied a little closer. Shifter or not, Garrett wasn't about to turn down comfort when offered, not when he needed it so badly.

A thought occurred to him. *Is Brian with Colletta of his free will? Drake said something about trafficking. People who can shift or do magic would be valuable. Did they get kidnapped too, and held against their will, sold off to the highest bidder?*

The thought made Garrett's stomach turn. He petted Brian, wondering how he came to belong to Colletta and whether he stayed out of choice. That made him sad, and he scratched Brian's ears again.

"Thanks for sitting with me," he said quietly. "I wish I could promise to get you out of this mess, but I don't even see how I'll get myself out. If I can protect you, I will."

Brian nuzzled Garrett's hand, and he took that for agreement. Eventually, exhaustion won out, and Garrett collapsed onto his cot, which was pulled up right beside Brian's so that he could keep a hand on the dog as they slept. *If we're both stuck here, at least we're not alone.*

CHAPTER EIGHT

DRAKE

*D*rake glared at his phone as if he could intimidate it into revealing its secrets. He had finally gotten a few minutes to himself around dinner time and missed Garrett. There was more work left to do, so getting together wasn't going to happen tonight, but he wanted to check in and see how the day had gone.

Except that Garrett didn't pick up. The call went right to voicemail. He waited half an hour and tried again, with the same result.

That seemed strange. Office hours were over, and Drake knew the clinic closed promptly. Even if Garrett had stayed late for some reason, he always picked up on Drake's calls.

Worse, he had a bad feeling about the situation he couldn't shake. That hadn't escalated to a vision, but it didn't bode well. Something was wrong, but Drake wasn't sure what to do. If he drove to the clinic and Garrett had just been busy, he might look like a controlling boyfriend.

Drake closed his eyes and concentrated. He and Garrett hadn't been together long. Psychic bonds developed over time, growing stronger. Still, Drake counted on the intensity of what he already felt for Garrett to help deepen his connection.

There. The impressions were faint but definitely belonged to Garrett. The intensity of the feelings nearly made Drake stagger. "Something's not right." *He's in trouble. Afraid. Angry. He's somewhere he doesn't want to be. Not sure he can get home.*

His phone rang from an unfamiliar number, and Drake hoped that for once, his sixth sense was wrong. Then he saw the text he'd missed.

Garrett: *Kidnapped. Car*

Before he could act on the upsetting text, he answered the call. "Hello?"

"Is this Dr. Thompson's boyfriend?" a female voice asked.

"Who is this? How did you get my number?"

"You've called the vet clinic several times lately, and I was with Garrett when he answered, and he said the call was from his boyfriend. I'm Kirsten. I work with Garrett, and I think he's in trouble."

FIFTEEN MINUTES LATER, Drake pulled up in front of a tidy house in a quiet neighborhood. A woman met him at the door. "Drake?"

Before he could answer, Bailey shot from the next room to bounce almost chin height, wagging and excited.

"Can he vouch for me?" Drake reached out to pet the dog.

"Come in. I think we've got a problem, but I don't know what to do."

Drake took a seat at the kitchen table and shook his head to decline coffee when Kirsten offered.

"Bailey comes into the clinic with Dr. Thompson most days. He's everyone's emotional support dog, and he really helps skittish patients and their humans." She reached down to pat Bailey and a pittie mix.

"Dr. Thompson hasn't done as much overtime lately… because he's been with you," she said with a tired smile. "Which is great. Really. He needs a life. We've all been nudging him to do something besides work. But he needed to get caught up, so I offered to take Bailey to the dog park with Cuddles and bring him back here. Doc should have picked him up two hours ago."

"Did you call him?"

She nodded. "Yeah. No answer—which is really weird. And the call went to the wrong voicemail. It's the one for when his phone runs out of charge, not his usual message."

Drake had noticed the response sounded different but didn't know there were two message boxes.

"I got a partial text. He's in trouble. Do you know anyone who would want to kidnap Garrett?"

"Kidnap? Oh, God. I was afraid something happened to him, but I thought that either he didn't have his phone, or it's broken," Kirsten went on. "He said you were some sort of cop. I didn't want to call the police because I don't have any evidence, but I was scared to drive to the clinic myself because of the guy who was in the other day."

Drake had interviewed a lot of witnesses. People always picked up on more than they realized, until questions led them to mention important details they had initially overlooked.

"Tell me about the guy."

Kirsten paused and chewed her bottom lip as if deciding how much to say. "We have this one client who gives me the creeps. The person, not the dog. The dog is sweet. But the man—we all think he's a gangster."

That sent a cold chill down Drake's spine. "Why? Has he done anything that suggested he was dangerous?"

Kirsten shook her head. "No. Except...I guess it's the vibes he gives off and the way he carries himself. Oh, and I know this is cliché, but I swear he's got a gun under his jacket from how it fits. You know, in one of those shoulder holsters like on TV."

"Do you know his name?"

Kirsten looked unsure. "I'm not supposed to breach client confidentiality."

Drake pulled out his badge. "Federal agent. I appreciate your dedication, but in the time it takes to get a warrant, Garrett could be in a lot more trouble."

"Mr. Colletta." Kirsten apparently decided to ignore confidentiality. "He looks like something right out of Hollywood, like an extra in one of those mob movies. He's always polite, but he gives everyone the creeps because there's just something...dangerous...about him."

Drake's heart sank. *Colletta? Shit. What's the likelihood that McElvoy's top enforcer is also Garrett's problem pet owner?* "I've always found it wise to trust your instincts on something like that," Drake replied. "He brings a pet to the clinic?"

"Brian. He's this big goofy boxer mix. Real sweetheart. And Colletta seems to take good care of Brian. So if he's a gangster, at least he loves his dog," Kirsten said.

"Do you think Colletta has something to do with Garrett not answering his phone? Did Garrett say anything that made you think he was in danger?" Drake clamped down on his worry and hoped he didn't have a vision in front of the witness.

"No, more of a gut feeling. Women's intuition," she said with a dry chuckle.

Bailey nudged Drake's knee and looked up at him. Drake ruffled his ears. He couldn't sense animal's feelings the way Garrett could, but he got the feeling that Bailey was stressed. Even Cuddles seemed subdued, sticking close to her friend.

"Can you give me the key or the codes to the clinic? And can Bailey stay with you until we figure this out? I can check on Garrett. Was he feeling okay? Maybe he passed out."

"He didn't say anything about not feeling well. He's been in such a good mood lately—and I think it has a lot to do with you," she replied. "He likes you a lot."

"He mentioned me?" Drake felt pleased and surprised.

"Don't worry—he didn't give away any secrets. He just said you'd had some fun dates, and you worked in law enforcement. So that's why I thought maybe you could help if he's in trouble."

"If you don't want to give me the keys, can you meet me at the clinic? Stay in your car until I call you. I'll make sure it's safe to go in."

"Yeah. Sure. I was hoping you'd say that. I'll bring my keys. I know the alarm code. We can be there in ten minutes."

"Thank you. I'll follow your car." Drake realized she couldn't see his truck and gave her a quick description so she'd know it was him. "Keep your doors locked until I call you back."

"Do you think he's okay? I'm totally all right if I've been overreacting."

"I hope so, but I've got a feeling something's not right. We'll figure it out." Drake stood and let her lead him to the door. The longer he talked to Kirsten, the stronger his worry became.

They made it to the clinic in record time, and he parked a block away. He cut through an alley to come around to the back of the building and saw Garrett's Suburban still in the small employee lot. Kirsten was there as well and gave a nervous wave.

So he didn't leave on his own.

No one else lurked in the parking lot, so Drake moved closer to the clinic. The overhead lot security lights illuminated the space enough to rule out most hiding places. Drake had his gun in one hand and a flashlight in the other, since most of the clinic was dark.

The kicked-in back door made ice settle in his stomach. He froze, listening. No sounds came from inside.

Drake could think of several reasons why someone might break into a vet clinic. Drugs and money were at the top of the list. But it didn't look like the place had been ransacked. As Drake moved farther inside, he realized most of the office hadn't been touched, not even the locked cabinets in the operating room.

Garrett's office, however, was in disarray, as if he had needed to pack quickly and leave in a hurry. Then he found Garrett's broken phone on the floor.

He wouldn't have left without this. And there's no reason for it to be broken—unless there was a fight.

He thought of Garrett's partial text about being kidnapped. Unfortunately, everything at the scene supported his worries.

The lights were still on in an operating room with a bloodstained surgical table. Someone had been operated on, but they left without cleaning up afterward.

Garrett's office also supported the idea that he had left in a hurry, with little preparation. His computer was still on, and his ledgers lay open on his desk. His backpack was missing.

Drake closed his eyes and laid a hand flat on Garrett's desk, hoping to pick up some psychic resonance that would explain what happened.

Drake didn't recognize the location. Shabby, like part of an abandoned building. Garrett didn't look hurt, just frightened and angry. Blood spattered his shirt, but Drake couldn't spot an injury.

Worst of all was the wash of despair he felt from Garrett, the acceptance that he probably wouldn't make it home alive.

Drake shook off the vision. His heart pounded, and his mouth was dry with the fear he picked up from Garrett and his own anxiousness to keep him safe.

Drake didn't touch anything, but he doubted the cops would get prints. He left everything as he found it and went out the back, then called Kirsten. "Do you have a way to view the security footage?"

"We should be able to see it at the front desk."

Drake cursed under his breath since the delay would cost valuable time identifying Garrett's kidnapper.

"You don't need to come in. The back door was open. Go home and lock your doors. Keep Bailey safe. After I've looked at the security footage, I'll call the police."

"Do you think they can help?"

"I don't think they're going to find anything useful in the clinic, but I want to see what showed up on the recordings. And thank you for being such a good friend to Garrett and Bailey."

"I hope you can bring him back safely. He's a great guy," she said. "I'll take good care of Bailey. He can have a sleep-over with Cuddles."

Drake took Garrett's broken phone and slipped it into his pocket. That was definitely withholding evidence, but Drake knew the local cops didn't have the FBSI's resources or his urgency.

I'm calling them for window dressing. I'm officially taking charge of this investigation.

He went to the front desk and figured out how to see the security camera footage, thankful that the system was fairly simple. Backing it up several hours, he saw Garrett in his office doing paperwork, then saw him startle as two men broke down the door and burst into his room.

"Oh, fuck." Drake hadn't expected to recognize Garrett's

kidnappers on sight, and he hoped he had been wrong about dog owner Colletta being the same as the mobster.

He called Clark. "We've got a big problem. Garrett's been kidnapped—and Antonio Colletta did it."

"Colletta? Are you sure?"

"Yeah. Just watched the security footage. He took Garrett. I got the license plate. Can you run it through the traffic cameras?" Drake gave Clark the plate number.

"Colletta works for McElvoy. McElvoy's outfit owns several properties in the warehouse district. I can run the plate and get a list of McElvoy's holdings," Clark volunteered. "Why would Colletta want to kidnap a vet?"

Drake ran a hand through his hair, trying to calm down. "One of Garrett's employees called me because he was late to pick up his dog. She said that Colletta's dog was one of their patients—the staff had him pegged as a mobster. It looks like they forced Garrett to do surgery and then took him—maybe for post-op care."

"There's a mob war on. Maybe they figured having a medic would come in handy."

"Yeah, that was my thought."

"We'll get him back."

Drake appreciated Clark saying so, but he worried that it might not be that simple. "Going to do my damnedest to make sure."

"Colletta has a pet vampire—Paul Bessette," Clark pointed out. "Don't forget to factor that into the equation. If he intends to keep Garrett against his will and have him cooperate enough to operate on their wounded soldiers, Colletta is likely to decide a little vampire compulsion will keep him in line. Less likely to cause brain fog than most witchy spells, damn near unbreakable."

Compulsion. The word made Drake go cold. His intuition told him Clark was probably right.

Colletta and McElvoy are neck deep in trafficking and the zombie drugs for supernatural creatures. Will they use something on Garrett to keep him from fighting back?

"Garrett doesn't know anything about the work I've been doing here or any of the players. It's possible that Colletta might have somehow found out about us, but since he had a client relationship with Garrett before, I don't think he took Garrett to get to me," Drake reasoned out loud.

"Safer for Garrett if Colletta doesn't make that connection, although with the vamps involved, this just got a lot messier."

"That's what I'm afraid of," Drake said. "We're going to have to factor a hostage rescue into the plans."

When Drake felt certain he hadn't overlooked anything in the vet office connected to Colletta, he called the police.

"FBSI Special Agent Drake Carlson reporting a break-in and abduction from a veterinary office," he told the desk clerk. "I'm onsite, so make sure they know that. The perps are gone."

He met the police with badge in hand, unsurprised at the frosty response from the senior officer. "You've already contaminated the scene," the cop groused.

"I'm claiming jurisdiction for the bureau," Drake told him levelly. "I called your office as a courtesy. We believe the abduction is related to one of our cases. That makes the veterinarian missing and endangered. When your team has finished here, I'll want a full report."

The cop clearly wasn't happy, but Drake didn't give a damn.

Drake's next call was to his boss. "We've got a change in the situation," he reported. "One of McElvoy's lieutenants took a hostage."

"Stick to the plan," Special Agent in Charge Walter Richards replied. "What do you know about the hostage?"

"Garrett Thompson, veterinarian." Drake forced himself to sound like he was talking about a total stranger despite his fear for Garrett's safety. "One of McElvoy's top lieutenants took his dog to the practice. After the last shootout between McElvoy's people and Rankin's mob, he took the dog to the vet after hours for treatment—and kidnapped the vet."

"Well, you don't see that every day," Richards said. "Do you know where they're holding the hostage?"

"Our best intel has McElvoy's operation down in the warehouse area. I did recon a few days ago, and what I saw backs that up."

"And Rankin's mob? Where are they located?"

"Farther out of town, another deserted industrial park," Drake reported. "Everything I've seen says McElvoy has the advantage, but Rankin isn't going down easily. I think they're headed for a war, and civilians—including the hostage—are going to be in the crossfire if we let that happen."

"What about the witch? The one who wanted to take over for Fletcher Swain?" Richards asked. "Your last report mentioned a couple of possible successors."

Drake gritted his teeth, straining for patience. He knew Richards liked to dissect the reports in person or on a call, but right now, Drake was mindful that every minute slipping away might be one less Garrett had to live.

"Jennings Weston is still most likely to take over. He's aligned with McElvoy and with Doane McGill."

"McGill's always been trouble. He and his brood have always flaunted being vampires," Richards growled. "Good thing the public is conditioned to think it's all a bunch of extreme goths."

"If we're sticking to the timeline, then I'd like to send a strike team in for the hostage at the same time the big fight goes down," Drake said. "McElvoy will use the hostage to his greatest advantage and then get rid of anything that slows him down."

He had to switch into the cold, practical place in his head where he went as an agent, forcing himself to talk about the hostage instead of Garrett, making it impersonal and tactical. There would be time for fear and heartbreak later.

"That increases the risk of giving away the whole mission," Richards replied.

"With all due respect, sir, it also increases the chance of bringing the hostage home alive." He paused. "You know the media will make hash of us if something happens to the hostage no matter how many mobsters and drug rings we take down."

He hated bargaining for Garrett's life like this, but he had a hunch how Richards's mind worked and where his sensitivities lay. Richards wasn't uncaring or corrupt—a nice change from Drake's prior assignment. Richards was just a little too clinical, forgetting the human element—and overlooking how something would play to the media.

"Simultaneous strikes," Richards finally agreed. "Go in after the hostage as the other teams attack. That provides cover and keeps the rescue from tipping our hand."

Finally!

"Three teams of five to go after the drug manufacturing, warehousing, and trafficking centers. One team of three to rescue the hostage."

He waited, hoping Richards didn't pick this moment to micromanage. Drake was relatively new in Richards's organization, but he had plenty of experience and recommendations around his leadership under fire and tactical skill.

"Your call. I'll send the teams—they'll be ready to go tomorrow. Anything goes south, don't get hung up on being a hero. Back out and try again another day."

"Yes, sir." What Drake felt wasn't relief, but being in

control of the solution empowered him to create a plan that didn't sacrifice Garrett for the larger objectives. He texted Clark.

Drake: *We're a go for tomorrow night. Come down ASAP to plan. Meet you here.*

He gave Clark his hotel address and then called the front desk and reserved two more rooms. Next, he reached out to Faye. "They've got Garrett."

"Oh, hon. I'm sorry. You got a plan to get him back?"

"A plan, the go-ahead from HQ, and fifteen agents, plus you, me, and Clark."

"I like that."

"I've got you and Clark rooms here at the hotel. Come down tonight—I'll order pizza, and we can work out logistics."

"I'll be there." Faye hesitated. "Drake—are you accounting for the vampires?"

Drake felt a chill. "I know Doane McGill is involved, and McElvoy has them on his team, working with his witch. What have you seen?"

"Not everything I see comes true."

"I know that. But I need full information to make good decisions."

"I saw a slender, dark-haired man sinking his fangs into the throat of a younger, blond man. The bite wasn't fatal. It wasn't a turning bite. But it creates a bond with the vamp— and if there's a witch involved, it can take away the will to rebel."

Garrett. Bassette fanged Garrett. I'm gonna—

Gonna what? End the vamp. But what does that do to Garrett?

"I'm not sure what that means. Will he turn?"

"Not if that's all there was to it," Faye told him. "As long as he isn't drained and doesn't consume blood at the point of death, he'll stay mortal. But what's been done is likely to affect his ability to fight the vampire or act against him. It may pose a difficulty with your rescue."

Would it make Garrett fight against me? I'm going to save him if I have to knock him over the head and carry him out, caveman style. I can apologize later. "How do I break the bond?"

"Either the vampire releases him, or you kill the vampire. If Colletta's witch is involved, there may be a hook to the bond—like if he leaves without being released, he'll die."

"Die?" Drake felt like he couldn't breathe.

"It's how they make sure their prisoners stay with them. Otherwise, a vampire's glamour would fade with time and distance. If there is a witch involved, the geas can have other stipulations as well."

"Okay. But do I have to kill the vampire and witch when I rescue the hostage? Can it be later?"

"I wouldn't wait too long. No telling what the limit is."

Drake paused, struggling for composure.

"They took your boy, didn't they." Faye didn't make it a question. He wondered how much her Sight told her about his relationship with Garrett. It made him feel exposed, but he also didn't feel judged, and he certainly wasn't about to explain or apologize.

"Yes. The only saving grace is—I don't think they know that there's a link between Garrett and me."

"Hmm. With a vamp who's bitten him, and a possible witch's spell, you can't count on them not finding out," she put his fears into words.

"Which is why I want us to go after him. You, me, and Clark. Closing down drug-making and stockpiling, holding trafficking victims—that's normal stuff for us, even with witches and vamps thrown in because we're the FB fuckin' SI."

"Language," she chided without a bite to her tone.

"The feds have a patchy history with hostages," he

defended. "They're a little too close to the idea of destroying the village to save it."

"Can't disagree with you. But we've got to think this through. You've either got to get the vamp to release him or kill the vamp."

"Not a hard choice."

"Easier said than done," Faye said sharply, "It gets tricky because we don't know how the witch is working with the vampire. And we probably won't be able to stop and sort it all out in the moment. Do you have a safe house set up for him?"

Drake's mind flashed back to the Carnival of Mysteries. *"You are safe here," Madame called after them. "Remember that when you need sanctuary."*

"I've got just the place." Drake prayed that he had not misunderstood. "People who will keep him safe while we figure out the details."

"Let's ride," Faye said. "It's been too long since I've raised a little hell."

FAYE AND CLARK gathered first thing in the morning, not long after dawn. Clark brought a couple dozen donuts, two large takeout jugs of coffee with fixings, and several bags of chips and cookies. He also had a couple of six-packs of soda and a bottle of whiskey "for medicinal purposes."

Clark was FBSI, with a background before that in law enforcement. He stood a little shorter than Drake, lean, spare, and strong. His close-cropped dark hair was starting to gray at the temples, framing sharp features, with blue eyes that didn't seem to miss any details.

Faye couldn't have been more different. Curvy and full of

energy, she only came up to Drake's chin, with naturally curly brown hair and inquisitive brown eyes. She was a few years older than Drake, closer to forty, and one of the strongest witches and mediums he had ever met.

Drake thought of Faye as a witch, but that generic term didn't really fit. She called herself a conjure, which was a combination of healer, far seer, medium, and someone who could call the natural energies and bend them to her will. Faye could hex and heal, speak to ghosts and compel them, track missing people, uncover hidden things, and make potions. She was also a damn fine shot.

Faye gave Drake a hug that nearly squashed his breath from his chest. Clark's firm handshake and a slap on the back acknowledged the same camaraderie. Faye unloaded a cooler with meat, cheese, and condiments for lunch sandwiches, a ham and cheesy potato casserole to be heated in the hotel microwave, as well as jars of her homemade sweet pickles and jams.

"And this is for celebrating afterward," she told Drake as she handed him a large jar of clear liquor.

Faye bustled around Drake's room, setting up a makeshift kitchen on his counter. "An army moves on its stomach. Gotta have fuel if we're going to war."

Next, she unloaded two boxes and set them on a braided rug she laid down. "I've got my conjure materials. Don't anyone step on the rug—it's warded."

They broke out the donuts and coffee as Drake took them through the information he had acquired. He couldn't sleep with Garrett in danger and only managed to nod off a few times before worrisome visions or the bleed-through of Garrett's emotions woke him. Since he couldn't rest, he researched and catnapped as much as he could.

"I found some drone footage of the whole warehouse area," he told them as he cast the image from his computer to the room's television. "It's a couple of years old, but I don't think anything major has changed.

"We think the traffickers are holed up in what used to be an old warehouse." Drake pointed out the two-story white brick structure. "This building was best suited for drug manufacturing." He drew their attention to a different building close by. "And from the floorplans we could find, this is the most likely to be where they're holding Garrett since it has a basement."

"I'll ask the ghosts to check. They're not happy with the people using those spaces," Faye replied.

"What are they telling you?" Clark asked.

Faye leaned back and clasped her hands on her lap. "Part of that industrial park was built over an old cemetery. People probably don't remember. But the ghosts do. Their bodies weren't moved—just the stones. They had something to do with the accidents and problems there over the years."

Drake remembered that the park had a higher than average share of worker injuries, safety issues, and property damage from floods and fire.

"I'm guessing that the ghosts liked the park empty, and mobsters weren't the kind of tenants they were hoping for?" Drake said.

Faye gave him the side-eye. "You think? They don't like the newcomers. The people who died at the site and who had been buried there were regular folks. They've done what they could to inconvenience the mobsters whenever they had the chance."

"Can you get them to confirm what I've just speculated from the drone footage?" Drake chafed at the delay. Going in without good information too far ahead of the other teams was suicide, but every hour that passed might be one less Garrett had to live.

"I can. Give me a bit. We're farther away from the site than I prefer, but they'll hear when I call."

Faye took a polished piece of clear quartz and held it in her right hand. In her left was an oval of amethyst. She closed her eyes and the others stayed quiet, watching her work and on guard in case something went wrong.

Expressions flitted across her face as if she was listening to multiple conversations at once. Clark and Drake had watched Faye work before, so they knew not to interfere, even when she looked concerned or distressed. Listening to the clamor of dead voices had to be difficult, and Drake didn't know how helpful the ghosts would be since they weren't recently dead.

Turned out, spirits have a long memory for grievance.

When Faye roused from her trance, Clark held out a cup of black coffee and took the crystals from her. Drake handed her a donut. Eating and drinking was good grounding after dealing with the spirit realm, and he figured that sugar and caffeine couldn't hurt.

"The ghosts haven't faded. They're even more angry at the mobsters than they were at the businesses, and they're happy to help however they can," she reported after she had drunk half the coffee and licked the sugar from her fingers.

"Jennings may be a witch, but he's ignored the ghosts, which works in our favor," Faye continued. "Then again, not every witch has a gift for spirits. If the vampires can see the ghosts, they've ignored them as well."

"How many witches? How many vampires?" Drake pressed.

"One main witch—that's likely Jennings Weston. A few lesser witches who do his bidding. Weston is only around some of the time. One of his disciples works for Colletta. Colletta runs a lot of the day-to-day show, and he has people who handle deliveries for the drug operation, deal with the trafficked people, and make sure the outbound drug shipments go where they're supposed to," Faye added.

"And the cops?" Clark's voice held an edge. Drake knew that there was no monster Clark hated more than a corrupt cop.

"The ghosts say no one bothers the people in those buildings." Faye shrugged. "So I'm guessing someone made *arrangements.*"

Clark muttered something under his breath. Drake didn't catch the words, but the disgust was clear.

"Any booby traps?" Drake knew the other teams would check for magical dangers, but it never hurt to have a heads-up.

Faye listened to her ghost spies, then nodded. "Not exactly booby traps, but wardings—not surprising with Weston and his witchlings around. The teams will need to put a damper on the alarm spells."

"And the vampires?" Drake asked.

"The young ones can't be out in daylight, and they're too groggy to be much use even inside the buildings until it's night," Clark pointed out.

"The older ones aren't as limited, but it all depends on whether they're loyal enough to the witches to risk themselves," Faye said. "Which I wouldn't count on."

"Are there other hostages besides Garrett? How many guards?"

Faye listened for a moment before looking up. "The guards come and go. They don't think there are other hostages—besides a dog."

"Anything else we should warn the other teams about?"

Faye shook her head. "They know we're going up against witches and vampires—and they can handle that. We'll have the ghosts on our side. If Colletta had a necromancer, the ghosts would have said so."

When they took a break, Drake stepped outside, going around the back of the building so he could be in the air without being easily seen. To his surprise, Faye joined him.

"I wasn't hiding from you, honest," he said, chagrined.

"I knew that. Something's troubling you. Perhaps I can help," she said.

"My boyfriend's been kidnapped by a mobster. Now it looks like there's a dark witch and a vampire involved," Drake replied, trying not to sound sarcastic. "And we're going into battle. Considering everything, I'm in pretty good shape."

She gave him a sad, kind smile. "You're wondering whether Garrett will come with you willingly or if he will fight to stay with the vampire."

Drake looked down. "Yeah. I know if he did, it wouldn't be his fault. Wouldn't be what he really wanted on his own. But still—"

"What will you do if that happens?"

Drake had been asking himself that question all morning. "Can you whammy him? I really don't want to give him a concussion in the process of rescuing him."

"By whammy you mean knock him out? I can't lift the compulsion. But I might be able to help him fight it, and failing that, I can probably make him pass out—harmlessly."

Drake nodded. "Okay. Good. I can work with that."

"Do you think they'll pursue him once we take him away?" she asked.

"Depends on whether we leave any of the bastards still breathing," Drake said. Before Garrett had been kidnapped, Drake was invested in stopping the drug smuggling and shifter psychic trafficking on their own merits. Now, he wanted to burn it all to the ground and make sure none of them walked away.

If the witches and the vampires put up a serious fight, his

teams could be left with no other option than scorched earth. Which was an even better reason to get Garrett the hell away as fast as possible.

"You getting any premonitions? Because my visions aren't telling me anything right now." Drake kicked at the asphalt with the toe of his boot.

"Can you pick up anything from him?"

Drake shook his head, miserable. "Just what I told you. He was afraid, then utterly terrified, and then—it was like a door slammed. I have to believe he's still alive, but I can't sense him."

"That's the vampire compulsion. It doesn't mean anything has happened to Garrett. It's a fog he can't break through. But if they believe he could be useful to them, they won't have hurt him otherwise. Hang on to that. Deep down, he's counting on you."

They ate lunch, napped as best they could to prepare for being up late, and studied floor plans, utility drawings, and construction permits for the rest of the day. Faye insisted they eat before the rendezvous time, and while Drake had no appetite, he wasn't going to argue with the witch.

Just before they headed to the industrial park, he handed Faye and Clark comm links like his own. He parked what he hoped was a safe distance away and got out of the truck.

"Rogers knows we're going in dark and quiet. But this way, you know what else is going on," he told them. They all knew their best shot at success—and getting everyone out alive—was making a quick in-and-out.

Drake checked his watch. "It's go-time. Good luck, everyone."

Clark went for the high ground with a sniper rifle. Faye and Drake stuck together. As soon as the old office building came into sight, Drake felt the temperature drop and a chill down his back that had nothing to do with the cold.

He caught glimpses of wispy figures out of the corner of his eye and darting flickers of light. Along with the cold came a wash of despair and anger—and the desire to mete out vengeance.

The empty business park had a post-apocalyptic feel to it, Drake thought. Boarded up windows, damaged roofs, and broken asphalt parking lots made it clear that the area was no longer inhabited.

The buildings were off the main road, back winding side roads, separated from more active areas. Perfect for not being noticed.

And if they've got the cops in their pocket, they aren't worried about routine patrols.

Clark found the spot he wanted inside, a stairwell looking down the steps to the basement, and gave them a salute as he peeled off.

Drake met Faye's eyes, and she gave a nod that meant her ghost squad was in place.

He had a long-bladed machete in his hands, another in a sheath on his belt, and a Colt .45 with a full clip in his shoulder holster. Decapitating vampires was a lot faster than staking them, and Drake didn't intend to waste time.

The ghosts plowed a path for them, flushing out three guards and setting on them with fury. Drake tried to ignore the men's screams as he and Faye eased past, relying on her invisible guides to find where Garrett was imprisoned.

Faye gestured, and the guards dropped to the ground. She looked at Drake and shook her head. "Not dead. Unconscious," she murmured. "The ghosts will guard the guards."

Drake couldn't sense Garrett in the usual way, but he had a strong feeling they were close. When two young vampires suddenly showed up blocking the way, he knew Garrett had to be nearby.

"You aren't supposed to be here," one of the vampires sneered.

"Technically, neither are you." Drake charged at the nearest vamp, machete raised, while Faye summoned a freezing cold cloud of ghosts.

Thanks to her distraction, Drake took out the guard closest to him, severing his head in one swing of the machete.

Ghosts mobbed the other vampire, and his eyes widened in terror as they attacked him, grabbing at his clothing and hair, scratching down his arms and face with sharp nails.

Before he could run, Drake swung again. The body and head fell in different directions, slicking the floor with blood.

Faye muttered under her breath. The ghosts became a gray, swirling shield in front and behind them as they moved down the corridor until they stopped at the door Faye had seen in her vision. She nodded, and Drake reached for the knob. Faye gestured, and the locked door swung open.

I wish she could teach me how to do that.

They burst into the room to find Garrett and a snarling dog trying to protect each other.

"Let's go," Drake said, intent on trying the easy way first. He stayed in the doorway, not wanting to spook Garrett.

Garrett swallowed hard and took a step back. "I…can't. Drake—get out of here before the guards come."

"Not without you."

"They won't let me leave."

"We aren't asking permission." Drake held out his hand.

Garrett looked ashamed. "I've been bitten—by a vamp. Not turned—"

"I know," Drake told him, meeting his gaze. "And I'm still here to take you home. We'll fix it."

"They put a spell on me. If the vamp doesn't release me, I die in three days."

"If you stay, you'll get killed in the crossfire, or Colletta will get rid of you when you're not useful." Drake knew they didn't have time to argue, but he preferred not to do anything that would hurt Garrett if he could avoid that.

"We can't leave Brian."

"The dog?"

Faye looked from the dog to Drake. "Not just a dog. He's a shifter—locked into dog form. He can't change."

Drake and Garrett looked in horror at the dog, who slumped, eyes focused on the floor as if he understood—and maybe he did, Drake thought.

"Wear this." Faye held out an amulet on a leather strap. "It won't remove the compulsion, but it will strengthen you against its influence, and it might slow the vampire's damage."

Garrett reached out and took the amulet, dropping it over his head.

"Can you feel a difference?" Drake worried now that he saw the effect the vamp had on Garrett, angry that the creature had taken away his free will.

"Some. Maybe. He said I'd die in a few days. I guess we'll know."

Drake felt the words like a body blow, but he tried to keep his face neutral, being strong for Garrett.

"We aren't going to let that happen. But we need to get out of here—now."

"Here—put this on the dog. Just in case." Faye pulled another amulet out of her pocket. Brian allowed Garrett to put it over his head, securing it with his collar so it didn't dangle too low.

"We need to go," Drake hissed.

They heard rifle fire outside. "Get moving—we've got incoming," Clark's voice crackled in Drake's ear.

"Roger." Drake gestured for the others to hurry.

Two more vampires appeared in the corridor as they headed toward the exit. Faye spoke a word, and an invisible force tossed one of the creatures several feet away, hard enough to crack the wall. He rose again and ran forward, only to be met with a tightly controlled stream of fire that set him aflame.

Drake braced for the assault, putting himself between the attacker and Garrett. He didn't expect Brian to lunge at the vampire, giving Drake the chance to step in and swing, taking off the creature's head.

More shots sounded. Drake urged the others to a trot, alert for trouble. Three guards who got in their way didn't slow them down. Drake shot two, and Faye dropped the other with a word.

"Head for the truck. I'll cover you and meet you there. If I get cut off, leave without me. I'll meet you back where we're staying," Clark told him on the comm.

Drake didn't like that plan, but he wasn't in a position to argue.

When they left the building, Drake heard gunshots and shouting and knew that the other teams were in mid-strike. He saw a couple of guards head their way, only to be dropped by sniper fire, telling him that Clark had found a new vantage point.

"Come on," he told Garrett and Brian, looking around nervously.

"The farther away I go, the worse I feel." Garrett looked like he was barely staying on his feet.

"Help him," Faye ordered. "I've got this."

Drake got under Garrett's shoulder, helping bear his weight as they stumbled toward the truck. Brian stayed right beside them and gave Garrett worried glances.

If Colletta is keeping him in his animal form, maybe he doesn't mind coming with us.

They finally reached the truck, and Drake breathed a sigh of relief. "Get in," he told Brian and helped Garrett into the back seat. Faye rode shotgun. Drake started the engine just as Clark jogged up and hopped into the bed of the truck. He pounded on the window, a signal to go.

Drake floored the pedal, despite the rough road, and silently apologized to Clark, who was stuck in the back. Faye watched for enemies ahead, and Clark had his rifle out, ready to cut off pursuit. Garrett lay very still in the back seat, and Brian stayed close to him, laying his head on Garrett's belly.

"I'm going straight to the carnival," Drake told Faye. "I'll take you and Clark back afterward, but right now, I want to see if they can help. And if they can't change anything, it's the safest shelter I can imagine."

"We've got your back. Do what you need to do," Faye reassured him.

Drake opened up the comm link and heard the team leads' voices, the organized chaos of a raid.

"Package picked up—making the delivery," he said during a break. "Going silent for now." He switched the link off and hoped the other teams had achieved their goal without losing anyone.

That was unlikely, but he still wished them the best.

"They've done better than hold their own," Faye told him. "They're doing what they trained to do. You need to focus on your mission. We aren't safe yet."

Hang on, Garrett. We'll see what the carnival can do to keep you and Brian safe and slow the curse while I go kill that fucking vamp and his witch.

One way or the other, we're going to be done with this.

CHAPTER NINE

GARRETT

I really don't feel good." Garrett leaned heavily on Drake as the world wobbled around him.

"We're going to fix that," Drake assured him. "Just hang in there. Stay with me."

Brian nudged against Garrett's thigh as if he was trying to guide him.

"Do you really think the carnival can help? Faye said she couldn't break the curse."

Faye confirmed that Garrett was both spellbound and under the vampire's compulsion. She hesitated to tinker with the way those magics twisted together unless there was truly no other choice.

The same was true for Brian. Faye figured out that he had been magically locked into his dog form. Brian mournfully nodded as if he understood every word.

"Faye said it could be broken—just not by her," Drake reminded him. They crossed from where he parked toward the ticket booth, leaving Faye with the truck. The carnival was closed. Its lights were dark, and in the moonlight, the tents and attractions seemed spooky, almost other-worldly.

"Why would they let us in? They're not open." Garrett was trying to follow a train of thought, talk, and walk without putting his full weight on Drake. It seemed like too much to juggle at once.

Back in his locked room, Garrett had felt a little off, like he might be coming down with something. Still, his mind had been clear. Leaving the room and building took a toll, no doubt a way for the vampire to keep his servants bound to him. The longer they were gone, the more fuzzy-headed and worse Garrett felt.

"Three days," he reminded Drake. "Spell and compulsion —remember? If we can't break it and the vampire doesn't release me, I'm out of luck."

Drake winced. "I'll take care of it, But I'm going to get you and Brian somewhere safe first. I can't fight if I don't know that you're safe. The carnival people might even know something we don't that would help."

"I don't want you to get hurt—or worse—saving me. I couldn't live with that," Garrett begged.

Drake looked at him, meeting his gaze. "And I don't want to live without you, so we'd both better get our shit together. 'Cos I'm pretty sure I love you."

Garrett caught his breath. He hadn't expected Drake to say that so soon, maybe not at all. "I love you too. I thought about that in the room. How I hadn't told you. Didn't want to die without saying it."

"No one is dying," Drake snapped. "Except for Colletta's pet witch and his fucking vampire. Don't talk like that."

Brian whined, and Garrett wondered how much of their conversation he could understand.

"Gotta help Brian too," Garrett said as they got closer to the main gate. "He's stuck. He deserves better. I'd tell him he's a good boy, but now that's kinda weird."

"You sound drunk." Drake took more of Garrett's weight.

"Drunk feels better." Garrett was certain that without Drake's help, he would weave and stumble. He had the sudden feeling that they were no longer alone. The man from the ticket booth appeared out of nowhere.

"We're closed. Why have you come?"

"Madame Persephone said we'd be safe here. I claim sanctuary for Garrett—and the dog." Drake didn't seem intimidated by the strangeness of their interrogator or the situation. "Please. Help him."

The man looked Garrett and Brian over from head to toe. "Hmm. Bewitched and compelled. Not something we see every day."

"Please," Drake urged.

Garrett turned to look at him and saw a vulnerability in his lover's expression that he had rarely glimpsed. Drake hadn't just come to rescue him from being kidnapped, Garrett realized. He had come to *save* him—even when that meant battling a witch and a vampire to do it.

"I will take you to Madame Persephone," the ticket man said. "Errante Ame will also want to know. There may be... repercussions."

"We don't mean to bring trouble on you," Drake said. "But I believe they'll be safer here than anywhere else. And when I stop the ones who did this, we'll all be safer."

The ticket man gave him an appraising look. "You believe you can?"

Drake nodded. "I can—and I will."

"Come inside. Madame is likely waiting for you." They followed him through the gate. Garrett didn't see any other security guards or barriers, but he felt a shiver of power roll over him as they crossed the boundary. He didn't want to know what it would have felt like without a guide and permission.

Without the bright lights and music, the carnival felt too

quiet, maybe even haunted. Stripped of its flash and color, silenced and deserted, the tents and midway seemed other-worldly, like a darkened gateway to another reality.

Garrett shivered. Drake shot him a look but didn't say anything, probably because the ticket man was close enough to hear. Brian stayed so close beside him that Garrett nearly tripped over the dog. *And here I'd been afraid he'd run off without a leash.*

His mind wandered, needing a focus so he didn't think about how totally screwed he was. His sympathy went to Brian. What was his relationship with Colletta before being cursed? Had they been boss and underling? Lovers? None of those seemed quite right, or explained why Colletta felt the need to bind Brian to him—or punish him by denying his humanity.

Yet Brian hadn't attacked Colletta. *Maybe a geas prevented it,* Garrett thought. And Brian had practically begged to go with Garrett when Drake came for him, so his loyalty to the mobster was definitely finite.

He thought about all the times he had talked to the dog shifter like an actual canine and cringed, although it hadn't seemed to bother Brian. In fact, Brian had acted completely dog-like, and had Garrett not had the new insight into the supernatural side of things, he never would have thought anything amiss—except for the mobster owner.

Did Brian become more dog-like the longer he remained without shifting back? Would he eventually lose his humanity or his ability to shift after too long? Thinking about Brian's predicament took Garrett's mind off his own bad luck.

"Almost there." Drake kept one arm around Garrett and a hand on his hip. Garrett didn't think he could stay on his feet without Drake's support.

"I'm sorry."

Drake barked a harsh laugh. "For what? Getting kidnapped? Being a doctor to a mobster's pet? You didn't even know the spooky side of life was real a month ago. None of this is your fault."

"I'm making your job harder." It took all of Garrett's concentration to talk. "You came here for a reason."

Drake stopped, letting the ticket man get a little ahead of them, and he turned to look Garrett in the eyes. "I came here to do a job. But finding you means everything. And I'm going to fight to keep you safe and keep what we have."

Garrett managed a watery smile but felt too fuzzy to say something profound in return, so he just kissed Drake on the cheek. "Love you too."

Brian nudged his leg, not wanting to be left out.

Garrett ruffled his ears. "You're the strangest mobster. I hope you're not a hitman."

Brian yipped, as if disputing that and Garrett managed a chuckle. "Okay. Good to know. Not a hitman."

Drake turned to look at him. "You sound really drunk. How do you feel?"

"Really drunk. But not in a good way. In a too much grain alcohol and not enough food way."

Despite everything, Drake smiled and shook his head. "When this is over, I want to know the story behind how you found that out. Vet school must have been more fun than I thought."

Ticket Man led them down the darkened midway toward Madame Persephone's tent. Garrett found it hard to believe that it hadn't been long since he and Drake had walked under the bright lights comparatively carefree.

Now, Garrett hoped he would live long enough for them to ever have another date.

Drake seemed to guess his thoughts. "Stop that. You can't

give up on me, Garrett. Nothing I do will matter if you give up."

"Not giving up. Need a rematch at mini-golf." Garrett did his best to put on a brave face, but he felt certain that Drake knew how scared he was, even without his psychic abilities.

Garrett could pick up Brian's feelings, although given his current circumstances his link was muddier than usual. Brian didn't seem at all sad at having fled Colletta's compound. Garrett picked up a mix of relief, fear, and resignation. He wondered if he would ever find out the story that led to Brian's situation, but being under a compulsion himself, he could sympathize.

"Madame will see you," the Ticket Man said, startling Garrett out of his thoughts. They stood in front of Madame Persephone's purple tent. Despite the darkness all around them, the tent shone with inner light.

"Seek your fortune wisely," he added before sweeping back the flap to allow them entry.

Just like before, Madame sat behind her table surrounded by cards and orbs. She looked up, and as her gaze swept over them, it felt as if she saw right down to their bones.

"I hoped you would come, but I did not know for certain. Please, sit down. Let me look at you."

Drake and Garrett sat across from her at the table. Brian stayed in the doorway as if unsure whether he was welcome.

Madame's expression softened. "You, of course you are. Come in," she told Brian, who padded over to sit close enough to bump Garrett's feet.

"You remembered my words." She looked from Garrett to Drake. "You came back."

"It seems...safer here," Drake said. "I need—"

"You need a sanctuary for your partner and the shifter while you go to war," she finished for him.

171

Drake nodded. "Yes. Can they stay? Will they be safe here? Can you heal them?"

Madame sat quietly for several minutes, eyes closed, with a meditative expression. Garrett wondered what she saw with her inner sight or whether she could read their thoughts or auras.

"Both are cursed." She opened her eyes. "It would be very dangerous to try to break the curses—if they could even be broken." At Drake's devastated look, she held up a hand. "But...I believe I can slow the damage, buy you time, ease the suffering. If there is no other choice, I will try to break it— but I don't think that would be a good idea."

"Can they be broken if I kill Colletta's witch and the vampire?" Drake's resolute expression gave Garrett hope even as it raised fear for Drake's safety. "I'm betting the witch is the same one who cursed Brian."

"Yes, although a violent breaking may not be comfortable for them. Such things are meant to exert control, a leash not easily slipped."

"But survivable?" Drake pressed.

"In theory, yes. I have not dealt with this particular curse before." She pointed to the amulets that Garrett and Brian wore. "A witch of considerable power made those. They stave off the inevitable. That witch could not do more?"

"She tried," Garrett managed, not wanting to sit there and have everyone else do the talking. "But no."

"First, I will send you to Peter, our potioner," Madame said. "Tonight, I want you to take whatever he gives you and rest. Tomorrow, if you feel better, I will introduce you to our performers who work with animals. They will welcome someone who can connect with their performing partners. We have our own medical people, but none who can hear what the animals are saying."

"I'm grateful to be able to stay here and for Brian to be

welcome. If I can be of help while I'm here, I'm happy to lend a hand," Garrett said.

"First, you need a good meal and a decent night's sleep—and so does Brian." Drake placed his hand on Garrett's.

Madame turned to Drake. "Thank you for trusting us with him. I believe you've left companions in your truck. These are not times to leave allies without defense. Go do your job. We will protect Garrett and Brian. May you find what you seek."

Drake walked Garrett to Peter the Potioner's tent and stopped outside. The Ticket Man gave them space, but he clearly followed to see Drake out.

"I'll be back as soon as I can. I know the time limit. I'm going to move heaven and earth to save you—and free Brian." He pulled Garrett into a kiss, and Garrett found himself feeling light-headed for a different and totally wonderful reason. He kissed back, trying to put all his faith and trust into it. When they stepped apart, breathless, he could swear Brian snickered.

"See you soon." Drake left with the Ticket Man.

Garrett forced himself to go into the tent with Brian close by his side. A man stood by a shelf of bottles filled with liquids in various colors and clarities. Peter had straw-blond hair that stuck out around his head like a scarecrow. That suited his thin build, all arms and legs, with a long neck, a pointy nose, and a prominent Adam's apple.

He looked up as Garrett and Brian entered.

"Welcome. I'm Peter. Madame told me to expect you. Come in. I can't cure you, but I should be able to slow the problem and make you feel more comfortable." His gaze dropped to Brian. "You, too."

Brian's tail wagged, and he gave a sharp yip of agreement.

"You can sense the curse?" Garrett asked.

"Yeah. We get a lot of that around here, people who need to be un-hexed. Messy stuff," Peter commiserated.

The way he moved around the tent reminded Garrett of a flittering wren. Peter motioned for Garrett to sit. Brian lay down beside him. Garrett felt grateful for Brian's support, glad they could stick together as strangers in a strange place.

The inside of the tent seemed larger than Garrett expected, and the strings of lights outside shone through the emerald canvas to give everything a greenish cast. Mismatched glass bottles filled wooden shelves, each one filled with mysterious liquids. The scent of ambergris and anise filled the air with a medicinal edge.

A large obsidian mortar and pestle sat on a narrow wooden table toward the back of the tent. Garrett saw arcane symbols etched onto some of the bottles, carved into the cable, and sewn into the tent fabric. The potion master hummed to himself as he moved around the tent, picking up bottles and putting them down again, finally selecting four containers and bringing them to his compounding table.

"I can create something to help you feel better—relieve the aches and fever, keep you from being miserable. Also something to give you energy during the day and sleep well at night, and to ease the fear."

"Anything is a help." Tiredness overwhelmed him, both body and spirit.

"It's not over yet," Peter said without turning back toward Garrett as he worked at his table. "Even strong magic can be unwound, and vampire compulsion is brittle if you know its weaknesses. As for your friend, he's experienced a terrible injustice. We'll see what we can do to make things right."

Brian nosed Garrett's ankle, and he reached down to ruffle the dog's ears. He resolved to think of Brian as a dog until things changed since Brian didn't seem to mind, and they both needed the comfort.

While he waited for Peter to create his potion, Garrett looked around the tent from his seat at the table. Some bottles had elaborate decorations pressed into the glass, while others were clear and unremarkable. He swore that the contents glittered and shone with an inner light, something he hoped was a trick of the candlelight. *It looks like something out of a fantasy novel. I hope his talents are as real as Madame's are.*

Peter returned after a while with a glass vial for Garrett and a shallow dish for Brian. Garrett's glass held a plum-colored liquid, while the green drink in Brian's dish looked less appealing.

"Medicines for supernatural creatures can be tricky because your metabolism and sometimes physical aspects aren't identical to regular humans. That means you need formulations that take those factors into account in order not to overdose or undermedicate."

That sounds like Drake's case, only those drug makers were illegal. If I get out of here alive, I wonder what I can do better for my clients who aren't what they appear to be.

Garrett shared a look with Brian and knocked the vial back, taking it like a shot. To his surprise, it had a blackberry taste that was much better than he expected. Brian bent his head to lap up the liquid in his dish. Whatever its flavor, the dog seemed to approve and finished it quickly.

"Thank you." Garrett hoped the potion would take effect soon and mute his symptoms enough to let him sleep.

"You are most welcome," Peter replied. "Now, you should both rest. I want to be able to check on you and hear if you have problems. I've set up a cot for you in the tent's side room. If you need me, I will know."

"Thank you." Garrett was grateful but completely exhausted. He only had the clothes on his back, so he followed Peter to the small side room right away. The cot, bedding, and pillow looked wonderful, and he appreciated the nest of blankets on the floor for Brian.

Garrett thought that he would lie awake, tossing and turning, but he fell asleep almost as soon as he lay down. Brian scooted the blankets closer to the bed, taking comfort in them being close to each other. Garrett didn't mind at all, feeling just as vulnerable.

"Drake will do everything he can to get us out of this," he told Brian. "I just hope he can find that vampire fast enough to count."

GARRETT WOKE to Brian nudging his foot with a wet nose, making it clear that Brian needed to go out. Garrett struggled to orient himself, then remembered escaping and making it to the carnival.

"Okay, okay. I'm coming," he told Brian in a sleep-heavy voice. He crawled out of the cot, stretched, and noticed a shirt and pair of pants lying next to the bed. He had worn his own clothes since the kidnapping; borrowing something fresh and clean was a godsend.

He dressed and slipped from the back room, wondering if Peter would be awake. He found the potioner already at work mixing elixirs at a work table.

"Good morning," Peter said without turning. "I trust you both slept well?"

"Out cold." Garrett was surprised that his rest had been deep and dreamless.

"Thank the potion. That's not all it did, but it is a happy side effect," Peter replied.

"Thank you for the clothes." Garrett looked down at Brian. "Where should I take him to do business?"

"Out behind the animal tents," Brian replied. "Turn left when you go out the door. You'll spot them. Then come back this way and keep going to the left, behind the midway. You'll see the area that's staff only—there's a shower and bathroom there and a mess tent. They know you're here, so no one will mind if you use the facilities."

"Thank you. Can I bring something back for you?" Garrett looked around but didn't see any plates.

"I'm fine, but thanks for offering. Go shower and eat. You'll both feel better. Come back here when you're done. I'll give you another dose of the potion. Rest is the best medicine for both of you. I've left a small stack of books for you, Garrett, to pass the time when you're not napping. And a couple of chew toys for Brian," Peter added with a smile.

"Thank you. I can't begin to repay your kindness."

"The carnival is here for those who need it," Peter answered with a slight shrug of his shoulders as if that should be evident. "Now go eat and get cleaned up. I'll see you soon."

Garrett rolled up the clothing and headed out, with Brian practically glued to his side. They found the showers easily. Brian guarded Garrett's clothes while he showered, sitting at attention outside the stall, clearly on duty. He declined Garrett's offer to give him a shower with a shake of his head, and Garrett wondered again how much human Brian had faded.

Getting clean and having fresh clothes made an amazing difference, perking Garrett up enough to realize he was curious and hungry. Brian led the way to the mess tent, and Garrett knew from what he could pick up of the shifter's thoughts that they were both in need of the comfort of a good meal.

He reached the door of the tent and hesitated, realizing that he lacked identification and was a stranger to the Carnival. Brian made a questioning noise, which Garrett interpreted as wondering whether he would be welcome.

"Come in, both of you." A man pulled back the tent flap. "Errante said you would be along. I'm Bill. If you need anything or have questions about the carnival while you're here, just ask me or my brothers."

"How will I know who your brothers are?" Garrett asked.

Bill grinned like Garrett had missed a joke. "Don't worry. You'll know."

Garrett entered the tent and looked around. It seemed bigger on the inside, and he was tempted to go back out for a second look, but the growling in his stomach made resolving his curiosity a low priority. The food smelled fantastic, a mix of familiar and intriguingly unknown aromas that heightened Garrett's hunger.

What is this place? A nexus between parallel universes? A wormhole between dimensions? I read a book series about a bar like that once, where time-travelers and universe-skippers could meet up and have a beer. Does time work the same here? If not, will that slow the curse's effects?

Now that he was awake and feeling marginally better, Garrett had a bunch of questions that hadn't occurred to him the previous night.

Would they answer if I asked? Or is it a need-to-know kind of thing? It's awesome—and kind of scary at the same time.

As odd as his sanctuary was, nothing about the people or the place made Garrett feel unsafe or unwelcome. He went through the cafeteria line with Brian plastered to his side, and people just acknowledged them both with a nod and a smile as if they were expected.

And maybe we were. Are they all psychic? There's definitely a vibe here that feels magical, otherworldly. Like we've stepped into somewhere that isn't quite our own world.

Some people were dressed as performers, while others

wore street clothes. As he moved through the food line, he was surprised to be handed a tray already loaded with coffee, juice, an omelet, bacon, and hash browns for him, and another plate of hash and a bowl of water for Brian.

"How—?"

The server behind the counter just smiled. "Keeps the line moving." He tapped his temple with two fingers as if to suggest a bit of mind-reading.

"How do I pay?" Garrett didn't see a checkout.

"Taken care of," the server said. "Enjoy your meal."

Garrett thanked the man and headed for a table off to one side where he and Brian wouldn't be in the way. Now that he had food in front of him, he realized how long it had been since he had eaten. He suspected the same was true for Brian.

"Bet you're hungry too." Garrett put the plate and bowl on the ground where Brian would be out of the way for people moving around the tables. Brian wagged heartily and dug in with gusto.

Garrett no longer felt surprised to find that his food was delicious and exactly as much as he wanted to eat. His coffee —just the right temperature and flavored perfectly with cream and sugar—hit the spot and helped banish the last fog of sleep.

He chanced a look around. Everyone *seemed* normal. He didn't see anyone who looked like a space alien or a talking creature. It reminded him of a Renaissance faire he had attended with friends where it was difficult to tell the performers from the costumed guests, and everyone spoke in a weird version of Middle English.

No one used an odd accent or antiquated speech pattern, but unlike that festival, Garrett felt like he had one foot through a portal to somewhere else. The vibe he picked up at the potioner's tent suffused everything, steady as a heartbeat.

When they move on, do they just poof out of sight and show up where they're going, or do they have to move like regular people?

It didn't surprise him as much as it probably should have when a young man came up to his table just as he and Brian finished eating.

"I'm here to take you to the animal area," the man said. "You're a veterinarian, right?" Brian nodded. "I'm Biff."

Garrett frowned, noting a clear resemblance between this man and the first one he had met, but also certain they weren't the same person. "But—"

"Oh, you met my brother, Bill. We're identical triplets. I guess our mother thought the names made it simple to tell us apart."

Garrett didn't think that made anything simple, but he nodded. "Thank you. I have no idea where to go."

"Don't worry," Biff told him. "At the carnival, you always end up right where you belong."

Garrett and Brian followed Biff out of the tent, where they passed another guy who looked just like him.

"That was Bob. You haven't met him yet," his guide told Garrett.

"Doesn't that get confusing?" Garrett asked.

Biff looked like the thought hadn't occurred to him. "You know, people from the outside always ask that. I guess it could, although it's always been that way, so we don't really think anything about it."

Garrett picked up a faint feeling of puzzlement and amusement from Brian and figured the shifter had followed the conversation. *Me, too, Brian. Me, too.*

As they neared the animal tents, Garrett could pick up a cacophony of thoughts, fragments that he could tell came from a variety of types of animals. Big cats like lions and tigers. Two bears. Dogs. Several of something small—ferrets, he wondered.

Brian made a small noise of distress. Before Garrett could reassure him, Biff patted the dog's head.

"Don't worry. Nearly all of the animals here are shifters or weres. We have a strict no-eating-each-other policy," Biff told them.

Brian only slightly relaxed at that, and Garrett bit back a chuckle. "Don't be afraid. I'll protect you."

They followed Biff into the huge tent. Garrett hadn't been sure what to expect, but the reality was more Dr. Dolittle than Ringling Bros.

Instead of stalls and kennels, one side of the tent provided comfortable and quasi-private sleeping quarters for humans, with a few nods to the animal alter egos. Right now, the performers were in animal form, going through their paces with the tricks that would amaze audiences. Garrett had always been in awe of ethical trainers who could get amazing feats from their herding and agility dogs, in part because most of those were true canines.

Coupling animal athletic capability with human under-standing took Garrett's breath away. His veterinarian training immediately registered that the performers were well cared for and seemed as happy as athletes and actors honing their craft.

"I hear you're a veterinarian."

Garrett looked up to see a man whose haircut and bearing strongly suggested animal trainer even though he wasn't wearing a costume.

"Yes, that's me." Garrett was unsure what Peter and Madame had been thinking when they sent him here. Garrett was sure the carnival's animals, both shifter and real, had excellent care, unlike with some traveling shows.

"Psychic?" The trainer tilted his head as if he was using his own skills to suss out the truth.

"More feelings and impressions than actual thoughts," Garrett admitted. "Is there somehow I can help?"

"And your friend is…complicated." The trainer gave a discerning look at Brian, who did his best doggie version of shrugged shoulders. "I'm Ronald, the lead trainer. Strictly behind the scenes. I leave the Big Top and the spotlights to the real stars." He swept his hand to indicate the animals, and Garrett sensed deep affection in his voice.

"Garrett," he replied. "And this is Brian. I'm not exactly sure why Peter and Madame sent me, but I'm happy to be of service if there's something I can do."

"Have you thought about catering to a paranormal clientele?" Ronald asked as they began to walk around the perimeter of the tent.

Garrett gave a grim chuckle. "I only learned there was such a thing recently. So I'm very new to that side."

"It's something to consider," Ronald said. "There have always been healers using magic and traditional cures like potions and salves. But there's an emerging field of prescription medications specially formulated for supernatural metabolisms. I imagine you noticed that your friend requires different dosages on regular dog medicine."

"Definitely. That's one of the things that made me question." Garrett had figured out how to make the medications he had work for Brian, but it required a lot of off-label applications and some very strange doses.

"We could use veterinarians who understand their clients without whisking them off to secret government facilities for experiments."

Garrett and Brian shuddered in unison. "That would be very bad."

"Right now, all the paranormal drug manufacture is underground—both good drugs and bad."

"That was the feeling I'd gotten." Garrett didn't want to say more from what Drake had told him.

"There are some efforts to create our own standards and inspection system, but it's just being developed. That would help a lot. The quality can vary, and that's dangerous."

Very dangerous. That would make it easy to over or underdose, and medicines that are cut with other, cheaper, ingredients can cause all kinds of side effects.

"The witches help a lot," Ronald went on, "but you can't always find one when you need one, and sometimes things don't go well." He looked at Garrett. "We—the paranormal community, not just the carnival—could use good people who are on our side."

Brian bumped Garrett's leg hard, and Garrett took that as agreement.

"I've always had an interest in chemistry. I took a lot of pharmacy classes in vet school because I thought being able to compound drugs for special needs was fascinating."

"We're about as special needs as it gets," Ronald said. "I've heard that shifters have a tough time out there because they can't go to a human doctor—the differences will get picked up right away and get the wrong kind of attention. So they go to vets and the treatment isn't usually quite right for the way we're different, but at least they don't get hauled away to a lab."

"I picked some of that up from Brian. There aren't any vet schools for paranormal creatures?"

"Not that I've ever heard of. Seems to be old school mentor to apprentice kind of learning, at least, that's what the carnival vets have said. Don't forget—our folks need to stay under the radar."

"Brian's...manager...just showed up with him one day," Garrett said. Brian grumbled something that Garrett gathered was highly impolite at the mention of Colletta. "No idea how he picked me off the internet. I couldn't figure out why Brian's baseline readings were so odd until I found out the truth."

"And it may have just been luck…but in my world, luck usually gets a nudge from something supernatural."

Garrett's mind spun, leaping ahead to the possibility of having an underground practice treating weres and shifters, with a small lab to do special formulations. The lab part would be highly illegal. *Then again, my boyfriend is a paranormal fed. Maybe we could work something out.*

Ronald looked at Brian with sympathy. "And then you get the sick fucks who pull this kind of shit." Righteous anger heated his tone. "They learn enough about the paranormal pharmaceutical side of things to brew up zombie drugs to aid control, compulsion, and curses. Bad witches, predatory vampires—they aren't all, but there are definitely some bad eggs—and the were-creatures' elders who want complete control."

Garrett had gathered as much from what little Drake had let slip, but apparently this was a bigger problem than he had assumed.

"I'm still wrapping my head around the idea of there being a supernatural underworld. My staff guessed that Brian's…keeper…was a gangster just because he fit the stereotype and the vibes he gave off, but we never actually thought we were right."

"Any time there's money to be made and people who need what they can't legally get, there will be someone willing to step in—for a price and a piece of the action," Ronald said. "But there are good guys too. Like the carnival. And the Federal Bureau of Supernatural Investigation, the Supernatural Secret Service, the US Supernatural Marshals—definitely on the down-low, but they're doing their best."

Like Drake, Garrett thought as the last of the missing

pieces clicked into place. *There's a whole parallel secret world out there, and most people will never—should never—know. I'm so lucky to find out—I just wish it had been under different circum-stances.*

Garrett suddenly felt woozy, and a stabbing headache made him double over. Brian was right beside him, protecting and comforting, as Garrett sank to his knees.

"Oh, dear. It must be the curse," Ronald murmured. Garett had the presence of mind to wonder how he knew, but then the pain interrupted his thoughts again.

"We need you, Errante," Ronald said softly as he reached out a hand to help Garrett stand. "Come on. I'll get you some water, and we'll wait for the boss to get here."

He supported Garrett's weight to walk to a chair and left him under Brian's watchful eye while he went for water.

Brian whined softly and nuzzled Garrett's arm. "Thanks. Guess I've been around when you've felt lousy. I appreciate you returning the favor."

After a thorough sniff and a lick to Garrett's hand, Brian sat squarely in front of him, making it clear that anyone who wanted to get to Garrett was going to need to go through him.

Garrett shut his eyes and tried to breathe deeply, hoping he didn't pass out. He felt the curse like a virus, making everything hurt and raising his temperature. Now that he knew about the zombie compulsion drugs, he wondered how much of his food and drink was laced when he was held captive.

"He's right here," Ronald said, and Garrett forced himself to lift his head and open his eyes.

He saw Ronald returning with the elegantly dressed, imposingly handsome man whom Garrett had glimpsed on his first visit. Despite the man's aura of authority, charisma—and power, Garrett didn't feel afraid, although Brian kept himself planted in front of the chair on guard until Ronald and the stranger arrived.

"It's okay," the newcomer said to Brian. "I'm here to help."

With that, Brian moved to the side and laid down so the man could approach Garrett.

"I am Errante Ame," the stranger said. "We met in passing but weren't personally introduced." Garrett couldn't help thinking that the man's voice sounded like he had spent a lifetime in the theater.

"I have," Errante replied with a chuckle, responding to the unspoken question. "Several, actually. But that's neither here nor there." His gaze raked across Garrett's form, and then he laid a hand on Garrett's head, only to withdraw as if he had been burned.

"Nasty bit of magic and compulsion there." Errante's glance turned even more sympathetic when he looked at Brian. "You, too, I see."

"Can you fix it? For either of us?" Garrett knew what Madame and Peter had said—and Drake's friend, Faye—but he couldn't help hoping.

"Unfortunately not without doing other damage," Errante said. "Which I suspect Madame also told you, but I understand why you needed to ask. I wish I could do more. But I suspect you are due for a potion and some of Madame's help."

Errante and Ronald got Garrett back to Peter's tent with Brian right beside them all the way. The potioner was waiting for them when they arrived.

"Bring him in." Peter held the flap back to the extra room. "I have a dose ready for him."

Garrett sank onto his cot and thanked Errante and Ronald for their help. The two men withdrew, and he heard quiet conversation, but he couldn't quite catch the words. Brian nuzzled him, worry clear in his eyes.

"Thanks." Garrett scratched Brian's ears. "You're a very good boy."

A vision overtook him, so clear and vivid that he feared for a moment he had been physically transported.

He saw Drake hiding behind a tall stack of pallets in a darkened warehouse. The air crackled with power, and a streak of blue fire lit up the gloom. Shadowy figures moved supernaturally fast, met by the crack of gunfire and the blur of steel blades.

The musty air stank of old rot and fresh blood. In the dim light, a battle raged, and Garrett guessed that Drake and his team had found the dark witch and the vampire who had caused so much mayhem.

More magic flared, setting the scene in hellish tones of orange and red. Garrett saw Drake drive a blade through a man's back, narrowly missing being hit by one of those bursts of flame. Drake threw himself forward, shoving the blade even farther into the man's body and sending them both stumbling into a third man, impaling him through the chest. Drake pivoted, bloody weapon raised, clothing and skin spattered with crimson, eyes wild, to face a new onslaught.

Blue lightning crashed all around, filling the darkened building and blinding Garrett so that he couldn't see whether Drake survived the battle.

The vision vanished, and Garrett struggled for breath. His body went rigid, heart pounding, lungs straining, and he thought he was going to die. Inside, it felt like his veins were being yanked out like roots from dirt, a fiery, blinding pain that denied him the relief of unconsciousness.

Vaguely, Garrett heard someone thrashing nearby and then the loud howls of a dog. Voices blurred with the rush of blood in his ears. Garrett felt hands grabbing him, steadying his body, and prying open his mouth. A thick, tart liquid slipped down his throat as the grip refused to let him turn his head or spit out the noxious potion. He struggled against the grip, trying to tear loose.

Suddenly, the torment stopped, and he slumped, still supported by the firm hold on his arms until he was eased to the floor. The vision faded. Garrett lay on the ground, utterly spent, gasping for air, head spinning.

Drake was covered in blood. Was he hurt too? Were those the witches and vampires? Did he win?

Garrett felt panic rise, fearing the worst since the scene had gone black, and he couldn't get the connection to spark again.

Could I see the vision because of my bond to Drake? And if I can't reconnect, does that mean he didn't survive?

"Easy, Garrett. Breathe." The gentle voice repeated those words over and over until he could slow his breathing and focus. He opened his eyes to find Madame kneeling next to him, looking worried.

Peter knelt next to a naked man curled into a ball on his side. *Brian?* Garrett managed to wonder as panic receded.

Errante Ame stood behind Madame and Peter, face upturned, eyes shut, arms outstretched downward, and hands splayed as if channeling energy through himself and sharing it with the potioner and seer.

Perhaps it was the aftereffects of the vision, but Garrett thought his whole body had a faint glow. With each breath, the pain faded, but the vision itself remained etched sharply in his mind.

"Drake's in danger. A witch. Vampires. Battle," Garrett managed.

"The curse and compulsion is gone from both of you." Madame's voice was both soothing and authoritative. "That means the witch and the vampire who cast the spells are dead. You're free."

Garrett focused on his body, looking for the signs of the

spell and the pain it caused. They were gone, leaving him feeling exhausted but completely normal.

"No, no, no, no!" Brian wailed, curled up in a tight ball. Peter brought a blanket to cover Brian, who now looked like a totally human young man with short dark hair, pale skin, and solid muscles. "I don't want this."

Garrett ignored his own vertigo to crawl close enough he could put a hand on Brian's shoulder. "It's okay. You're safe. And you aren't locked in anymore."

Brian turned to him with wide eyes. "You don't understand. I don't want to be human again. I wasn't a good man. I did things...I was a bad person. Colletta had me bound as a punishment, but it was the best thing that ever happened to me. I'm a much better dog. Please, let me be my dog again—permanently."

Garrett saw a look pass between Errante and Madame. Errante came around to look Brian in the eyes. "We can make a cleaner binding than what was done before, one that won't cause you discomfort. But it will be permanent. You'll gradually lose your human memories and become fully dog, and your lifespan will be closer to dog than man."

"I don't care." Brian sounded miserable. "Please just let me be my dog."

"You can come home with me." Garrett realized he had grown very fond of dog Brian. "I have another dog, Bailey. I think you two will get along. I promise to take care of you."

Brian looked at him with the gratitude Garrett had seen many times in his dog's gaze. "Thank you. Thank you so much—for everything."

Peter came back with a goblet filled with a blue liquid and handed it to Brian. "Drink this. It will help the magic go more smoothly."

"I'm ready." Brian knocked it back, barely wincing at the taste.

Errante and Madame placed their hands on Brian's head. Errante's mouth moved in a silent spell. Madame closed her eyes, and her face took on a look of intense concentration. The air blurred around Brian, and he took on a golden glow. When the light faded, he was his dog-self once more.

Brian shook off, walked several quick circles, and sat, tail thumping. He came over to Garrett and bumped his hand, and Garrett smiled, scratching his ears.

"I guess Bailey's going to have a new friend." Garrett grew serious again, remembering the vision.

"I saw Drake fighting witches and vampires, and then our spell was broken. But I can't feel our connection anymore. I'm afraid of what that means."

Madame closed her eyes, concentrating. "That future is not clear. It may not yet be decided, or it may not be mine to see. Don't lose hope. I sensed the bond between you. You are soulmates. He will come back to you if it is within his power to do so."

Garrett murmured his thanks for her effort, but cold dread seized his heart. *She can't see if he's dead or alive. I'm grateful that he fought to free Brian and me and to keep others from being hurt like that, but I want Drake to come back to me. Please let him be alive.*

"Both of you have been through a lot." Peter looked from Garrett to Brian. "I asked Bill to bring dinner for you. Eat, then sleep as long as you can. It wouldn't be wrong to sleep an entire day, given what you've had to deal with." He offered a kind smile. "Don't lose hope. A lot can happen in a day."

Garrett thanked them all, feeling his energy fade. He felt the absence of the curse and the vampire's compulsion like a break in a fever or the healing of a bone-deep ache. Now, he was completely exhausted from the ordeal and heartsick with worry for Drake.

He didn't know which of the triplets brought the food,

but he thanked the man profusely. Garrett didn't think he would have an appetite, but he found himself ravenously hungry and thought the food tasted amazing. He wondered if that was a magical incentive to eat for his own good, or whether a combination of anxiety and the physical demands of being healed stoked his hunger, but he ate everything, as did Brian.

"Sleep," Peter said. Once they were assured that their intervention had succeeded, Madame and Errante had left while Garrett and Brian ate. "No harm will come to you. If we learn anything about Drake, I will let you know."

Garrett retreated to the side room and sprawled on his cot. Brian nested in a blanket on the floor, within reach of the cot.

Please let Drake be safe, he begged the universe. *Please bring him back to me. I just found him. I can't lose him now.*

As Garrett drifted off, he kept Drake's face in his mind, remembering his voice, his laugh, and his touch. *I love you. We've just started to find each other. Don't leave me.*

CHAPTER TEN

DRAKE

*L*eaving Garrett behind at the carnival was one of the hardest things Drake had ever done. Everything in him wanted to remain close and protect Garrett, helping him through his ordeal.

Knowing that he could end Garrett's pain by killing the witch and vampire who cursed him was barely enough to tear Drake away when each step felt like a betrayal.

Drake switched into what he thought of as cop mode, shoving down his emotions and focusing solely on the job. He hated having to operate like this, but it kept him rational and undistracted even when everything crashed down around him.

"Warehouses suck," Drake muttered as his team spread out. HQ had sent six operatives, three of whom were witches, although none were as powerful as Faye.

If Paul Bessette and Colletta's witch had been smarter and less convinced of their invincibility, they would have skipped town once they realized the FBSI was onto them. McGill and Weston had apparently taken the hint and left.

But like villains who never learn not to monologue,

Bessette and Colletta's witch were sure they were smarter and stronger, and that McElvoy had their back with the powers-that-be.

McElvoy had already sold out everything he knew in exchange for immunity for himself and his coven. Even as Drake led the raid, the FBSI operatives were sorting through financial records, recorded phone calls, emails, and occult Darke Web stuff—the ensorcelled encryption online network used by many in the supernatural community—that wasn't as hidden as its authors supposed. Rankin and his witchlings had vanished before the FBSI could catch them, but that was a problem for another day.

Warlock Willis Osborn's illicit empire was finally being permanently disassembled, and the wanna-be successors destroyed. Even the remnants of Swain's network were being crushed. McGill and Weston were fugitives, not the supernatural power brokers they fancied themselves. HQ already had their assets and accounts located and locked down, and their main lab had been seized and its chemists arrested.

It was game over, except Bessette and Colletta's witch didn't know it yet—or if they did, they had resolved to go out swinging. Drake didn't know which was worse—the two of them fighting to hang on to something they didn't know they had already lost or making a doomed last stand resolved to take as many of their enemies with them as they could.

When Drake's team was done tonight, the vampire and witch would be dead or in custody.

And if the universe smiled on him, Garrett's curse would be removed, he would be alive and well, and they could live out their lives together.

In Drake's experience, the universe rarely smiled.

"Go."

That word, spoken into the comm link, unleashed the onslaught.

Faye led the witches, who sent up a synchronized burst of magic, creating a dome over the warehouse and locking them all inside.

"Now."

The warehouse sprinklers turned on by magic, sending down a rain of blessed water laced with salt and colloidal silver. It didn't bother the witches or the FBSI agents, but Drake counted on it blistering Bessette's skin and weakening any vamplings he might have hidden in the recesses of the old building.

Screams drew the agents to the vampires' hiding places. They opened fire with automatic weapons, sending a hail of silver-tipped bullets into the shadows where their scanners indicated colder-than-normal bodies without heartbeats.

Bleeding, skin peeling, shrieking, the vampires attacked, driven mad with pain and fury. Some ran into the gunfire. Others, still wily despite their injuries, melted into the shadows and circled, coming at the team from all directions and descending from above.

One of Drake's team suddenly vanished into the air, grabbed by a vampire who held him aloft as he bit into the man's neck, using his body as a shield. Drake took advantage of the monster's momentary distraction as he feasted to shift positions and fire, sending round after round into the vamp, forcing him to drop his meal.

The dead vampire fell, landing next to the slaughtered agent.

The rest of the vampires charged, resolved to take as many attackers with them as they could if escape was not an option.

The witches left their dome intact but fought a pitched battle against Weston's witchlings, trading bursts of lightning and repelling curses.

Drake glimpsed movement to one side, away from the

main battle and closer to the door. His witches had assured him that the building was sealed, not to be exited without the removal of their spell, but Drake didn't expect Colletta's witch and Bessette to let that stop them.

He circled, watchful and wary. His premonition looked exactly like this—the warehouse, the witch battle, and now, slipping between pallets and containers to confront his quarry.

When Bessette rose in front of him, fangs bared, Drake was ready. He fought down mortal panic, dodging at the last second to avoid the vampire's sharp teeth. The vamp tried to throw him across the open space, but Drake held on, merely tumbling away.

He came back up at full power and sank his machete into Bessette's back.

"No!" the witch shouted and raised a hand to send a killing spell in Drake's direction.

Drake shoved forward, using Bessette's body as a shield, and rammed the protruding blade into the witch's chest with his full strength.

He hung on to the handle, ducking behind Bessette's form, and braced himself for pain, expecting to be incinerated.

Runes carved into the blade kept the witch from lobbing a death curse, freezing his magic as the knife stilled his heart. Bessette's corpse was already starting to rot, long overdue and preserved only by his vampire nature.

As Drake drove the killing blow home, everything went bright white for a second. He glimpsed Garrett drop to his knees and clutch his chest in agony, then topple to the side and lay still.

Garrett!

With his dying breath, the witch scraped together enough feral magic for a final strike, sending Drake flying across the open space so that he landed hard and painfully on his back. That knocked the wind out of him, and he braced for the witch to follow and kill him, but the witch sank to the ground beneath the vampire's disintegrating corpse.

Stunned by having the breath knocked out of him, but more from the glimpse of Garrett, Drake stayed down.

Was Garrett too linked to the vampire and the witch? Did killing them kill him?

I did my job. Did it destroy my lover?

"It's over. You'll be glad to know I took out Colletta myself." Clark reached down to offer Drake a hand, and Drake took it, pulling himself upright. "They're all dead. Fancy of you to do a two-in-one."

"Yeah, that's me. Fancy." Drake barely listened, heart breaking as he searched for the nascent bond between him and Garrett and found only silence.

Were we too slow to save him? Did we miss something about the witch's magic that was a poison pill, killing him if the witch died? Was the vampire's compulsion even stronger and faster than he knew?

I've won the battle—and lost what mattered most to me.

Bodies littered the floor. Faye and the allied witches spread out, removing dark magic sigils and wardings like a supernatural bomb squad.

"Sound off," Drake ordered on the comm link, counting as the agents checked in and coming up one short. "Nolan. Where are you?"

"I saw Nolan fighting a vamp over in the rear quadrant," a voice spoke up. "Haven't seen him since then."

"Shit," Drake muttered. "Go check. Report back."

A few minutes later, the link crackled to life. "We lost Nolan. Bastards dropped him from the ceiling."

Drake wanted to give in to heartbreak, but his team needed him, and that kept him on his feet.

There will be time to fall apart later. Time to grieve.

A thorough sweep of the warehouse confirmed that Weston's witches and McGill's vampires were all dead. Nolan was the only casualty from Drake's team, fulfilling the vision he'd seen. Weston and McGill had fled before the battle and were in the wind.

"Team Three, reporting," a voice said in his commlink. "We cleaned out the vamp nest. They were weak as fledglings. Got them with silver, and burned it all down. They're toast."

"Good job," Drake replied mechanically. He wondered if McGill had intentionally sacrificed his weaker vamps.

Faye and Clark joined him. The look in Faye's eyes told Drake that she understood his fear for Garrett.

"Weston never had many witches, and none of them were very strong," Faye told him. "He was always afraid of rivals and power struggles. All the ones who stayed to fight died, especially since Weston didn't stick around to lend them power. We'll locate the others by following the energy they're bleeding."

"Looks like your intel paid off," Clark said. "I can handle the cleanup and keep you posted. You've got somewhere else to be," he added with a pointed look.

"Thank you." Drake knew that his ragged voice betrayed his worry. "I just don't know what's waiting for me when I get there."

"He's not dead."

Drake pivoted to look at Faye. "What?"

"You heard me. He's not dead. Plenty of messy magic getting thrown around, and I don't know details, but Garrett's alive. Go. Find out what happened—because whatever mojo got worked on his end definitely undercut Colletta's witch here."

Drake thanked them and checked in one last time with

the other teams, who also had the job under control. Leaving Clark and Faye in charge of the cleanup, Drake ran for his truck and drove into the night, heading for the carnival, praying to anyone who might listen that the fight hadn't been for naught.

Drake reached the festival grounds and screeched to a stop, slewing sideways in his rush. He ran toward the gate, heart pounding, fearing the worst.

A tall man dressed in black stepped out from the ticket booth. "You are expected. Enter—and may you find what you truly seek."

Drake mumbled his thanks and sprinted past, remembering the path to the potioner's shop even in the darkened maze of the closed carnival.

Without the lights, music, and garish colors, night-washed to gray, the carnival felt even more other-worldly, a place in between realities. Absent the distraction of gawkers and patrons, he could sense the subtle, powerful currents of strange energy that wove through the faire, giving it a life of its own.

"I'll take you to Garrett." A dark-haired man stepped from the shadows. "I'm Bill. Follow me."

Drake clung to Faye's reassurance, hoping his psychic senses would confirm that Garrett lived. He recognized the path and saw the potioner's tent ahead.

"He's waiting for you," Bill said, and Drake wondered if the man was psychic or just guessed his thoughts. "We've all been waiting."

Drake wanted to ask about Garrett, but the words stuck in his throat. Now that he was only minutes away from seeing for himself, the question seemed moot.

We killed Bessette, Colletta, and his witch. Jennings Weston and Doane McGill escaped, but Willis Osborn's and Fletcher Swain's organizations are finally dismantled. Their witches and vampires are dead or fled. But I've lost everything without Garrett.

"Please, come in," Peter pulled back the flap, allowing Drake to enter. Bill exchanged a nod and went on his way.

"Where—"

"Over here." Peter led him to a small side room and motioned for Drake to go in. "If you need me, I'll be out here."

Drake gathered his courage and stepped inside, braced for whatever awaited him.

"Garrett?"

Garrett lay on a cot covered with a blanket. Brian lay on the floor beside him, and the dog raised his head as Drake entered, then poked Garrett with his snout.

"What—" Garrett blinked a couple of times and looked at Drake. A tired smile lit up his face. "You're here. You're alive."

Later, Drake wasn't sure which one of them moved first. He suddenly had Garrett in his arms, warm and alive, and drew him in for a long reunion kiss.

"I was so worried." Drake buried his face in Garrett's hair and took in his scent. He smelled of herbs and candles and potions, and Drake couldn't get enough of it.

"So was I." Garrett nuzzled closer. "I saw what happened —at the warehouse."

Drake frowned, pulling back enough to see Garrett. "You *saw* it?"

Garrett nodded. "It must have been our bond because that's not my usual sort of connection. I saw you put a blade through the vampire and shove it into another person. But there was so much blood, and then it all went dark, and I couldn't sense you anymore. I was afraid you didn't make it." He sniffed back tears, and Drake kissed him gently.

"It was the same for me. When the curses broke, I got a glimpse and saw you fall, but after that, nothing." Drake combed his fingers through Garrett's hair and ran his hands down his arms and back, reassuring himself that Garrett was solid and alive.

Drake suddenly realized that Brian lay curled around his feet—in dog form. "What happened?" Drake was sad that they hadn't been able to free the shifter.

"The curse broke," Garrett replied. "But Brian begged to be locked back in his dog. So now he will be a dog for the rest of his life and eventually forget being human." He cleared his throat nervously. "I promised to take him in."

"Of course," Drake replied, and Garrett looked up, surprised and happy.

"You're okay with that?"

Drake shrugged. "I've heard way weirder dog rescue stories." He reached down and patted Brian's head. "After all, he's a very good boy."

EPILOGUE

GARRETT

Six months later.

"The last of the equipment that you requested came in today." Drake hung up his jacket and set his messenger bag aside. "That should be everything you need for your lab."

Garrett pulled his boyfriend into his arms and hugged him tight, ending with a passionate kiss. Bailey and Brian circled their legs, tails thumping, just like every night at dinnertime.

When Drake stepped back, he made sure to pet both dogs before toeing off his shoes in the entry hall. "How did you beat me home today?"

"It was quiet at the office," Garrett said with a shrug. "Brian and Bailey helped me make the rounds, but we didn't have any last-minute emergencies, so I spent a lot of time working up plans for the lab."

Formulating pharmaceuticals without FDA approval was illegal. But gaining the okay from the newly-created Federal Supernatural Drug Administration gave Garrett and a couple of carefully cleared assistants the go-ahead to work on creating variants of public domain medications specially formulated for creatures with paranormal metabolisms.

"If we can prove the concept, this is going to be big." Garrett went to the counter to dish out spaghetti and meatballs from a large pot. "Pain killers, anti-inflammatories, heart meds—if we can adjust for the differences between humans and shifters, vampires, and were-animals, we could relieve a lot of suffering and improve overall health."

"And from the FBSI side, it also dramatically cuts demand for the illegal, unregulated paranormal pharmaceuticals, which makes dealing less profitable." Drake poured glasses of water for them.

"If we can get approval for the quality control measures I'm working on, patients don't have to worry about getting under-the-table crap that is dangerous or doesn't work," Garrett added.

"Any luck on better tests for rougarou roofies and monster meth?" Drake portioned out food for the dogs as he talked.

"I'm trying to figure out how to test for the zombie drugs like Colletta originally used on Brian," Garrett replied. Brian didn't flinch at the name, and Garrett was glad for him that apparently, the worst memories had been forgotten.

"That's going to be a huge help," Drake said. "We get shifters and creatures into custody, and we can tell something's not right, but we don't have good tests to figure out what, let alone being able to handle an overdose."

"You know, I heard about drugs that could put a *person* under a compulsion—like the zombie legends—but it never occurred to me that would be a problem with supernatural creatures, even after I found out they existed."

Garrett dug into his food between comments. Drake leaned in to wipe spaghetti sauce from his lips.

"How's your network of vets in-the-know taking shape?" Drake asked as he put down food for Bailey and Brian. They ate separately and didn't steal from each other—much.

Just in the time since that night at the carnival, Garrett could tell that Brian's humanity was slipping away, replaced more and more by dog-ness.

Drake had found records of Brian's human life. Hardscrabble upbringing and petty crime had escalated to bigger things, attracting the attention of McElvoy's mobsters. Drug running, assault, arson, grand theft, and several possible murders gave Garrett deeper understanding as to why Brian didn't want his human life back. If he didn't die in a gang fight or a bust, he'd have ended up in prison.

He really was a hitman. Imagine that. When Brian looked up, tongue lolling, grinning wide with his tail thumping, Garrett knew Brian had made the right choice.

Bailey had always been intrigued when Brian came into the office with Colletta, and now that he lived with them, Bailey accepted the change and made Brian his new best bud.

"I'm slowly getting quiet referrals to other vets who have been secretly treating shifters, weres, and other creatures all along." Garrett placed bowls of salad at their places on the table. "The shifter communities have been especially helpful. And here I thought I was the only one."

"I'm still adjusting to shifters needing a designated fake owner to take them to the vet," Drake replied as they sat to eat. "Good thing that falsifying dog licenses isn't a major crime."

"Your friends who busted Swain's operation put me in touch with a shifter community in New York that's been very helpful." Garrett poured ranch dressing on his salad.

"Some days, I still feel like I fell through the looking glass. I never believed supernatural things existed, and now I find out there's a very large, well-connected community out there with all kinds of parallel services. It's mind-blowing."

"I'm amazed that no one's done what you're doing long before this," Drake replied. "In hindsight, it's obvious."

"It did get done—one vet at a time, passed along by word of mouth, kept under the radar," Garrett said. "As long as it could be excused as compounding for individual patients, they weren't likely to have the DEA breathing down their necks. Just a little special formulation for unusual cases. Vets usually are the pharmacy for their patients for specialty medicines, so it worked—or at least, it was better than nothing."

Garrett knew now that when it didn't work, shifters and other creatures bought unregulated medications on the street, with all the dangers that entailed.

"You're the perfect person to take point on this," Drake noted with his mouth full. "You've got cover from FBSI in case any mundane agencies come sniffing around. You've got vet and pharmacy credentials, so you know what you're doing—without needing a big lab and a bunch of experiments."

Garrett shuddered. "Yeah, no. Experiments aren't happening on my watch. If I need to test something, I can get consent from the subjects themselves. No one gets hauled away to a secret government lab."

As far as his regular clinic staff knew, nothing had changed except that the creepy mobster client never came back, and Brian now lived with Garrett. He kept the lab project completely separate and secret for everyone's safety, but his supernatural clients benefitted from the drugs he altered and what he learned in the process.

As word got around, Garrett saw an increase in shifter and were clients, with his staff none the wiser.

"I'm thinking of creating a mentoring program down the

line," Garrett said as he tore off a piece of garlic bread. "We can't exactly open a vet school, but trial-and-error is dangerous, and it's also dangerous to look for info on the Darke Web. The feds could be listening," he added with a wink.

"I think that's a great idea—but don't forget to be home now and then." Drake slipped his hand onto Garrett's and stroked his knuckles.

"Oh, I have plenty of incentive to come home—especially when my secret agent boyfriend isn't out gallivanting," Garrett flirted shamelessly.

Drake and Clark's territory encompassed both Moundsville and Wheeling, as well as surrounding areas. They only had to go into headquarters a couple times a month, and many of their meetings had moved to secure online platforms.

That made the decision easy for Drake to move in with Garrett. Sometimes work took him into the field for short periods, but most days, he was home at night with Garrett and the dogs, which made Garrett extremely happy and was thoroughly approved by Brian and Bailey.

"I gallivant as little as possible these days." Drake nudged Garrett's knee under the table.

They made quick work of cleaning up after dinner and tangled together on the couch afterward to catch the newest episodes of a few favorite series. Garrett found it difficult to concentrate on the show pressed up against Drake, and he felt his body react to Drake's scent.

Garrett lightly ran the flat of his palm down Drake's arm and felt the other man shiver. He mouthed at the back of Drake's neck and blew across his ear, then traced its shell with his tongue.

Drake shifted to push his ass against Garrett's groin. Garrett pressed his hard-on between Drake's ass cheeks, making his arousal clear.

"Want to move into the bedroom?" He slid his hand down to cup Drake's erection and stroked him through his jeans.

"Thought you'd never ask."

They stopped the show and switched to a music channel, then Garrett led Drake toward their room. He paused at the door and looked down at Bailey and Brian.

"Sorry, guys. This is private stuff. You can have the whole couch all to yourselves," Garrett told the dogs, who dutifully retreated as he closed the door.

"Now, where were we?" Garrett mused aloud, turning Drake to face him and running his hands up Drake's chest, capturing Drake's mouth with his own.

"Didn't know spaghetti made you horny," Drake quipped. "If that's the case, I vote for pasta every night."

"*You* make me horny." Garrett pulled Drake's T-shirt over his head before stripping out of his own. They both shimmied out of their pants and briefs, and Garrett tugged Drake to the bed.

"Been thinking about this all day," Garrett confessed, pulling Drake in for a long kiss with plenty of tongue and lots of groping.

"I like the way you think," Drake managed when he came up for air.

"I've been reading those romance books." Garrett kissed his way down Drake's neck, then teased at his nipples. "Figuring out what I want to do with you."

"And what did you decide?" Drake sounded breathless, and his cock stood at attention, hard and leaking.

"Everything. I want to do everything with you."

Drake kissed him. "I love that—and I want to do everything with you too. Just realize we're not teenagers anymore. So probably not all in one night."

"We could go on vacation, not get out of bed all week," Garrett teased, working his way down Drake's body with his mouth and hands. He stroked his fingers down Drake's back and slipped them down his thighs to push his legs apart far enough that Garrett could go down on him in one move.

Drake moaned and lightly tangled his fingers in Garrett's hair, leaning back and spreading his legs.

Garrett worked Drake's cock like he had practiced on a dildo he had bought, doing his best to remember the tricks he had seen in some of the videos. He slipped his hand between Drake's legs, palming his balls, then stroked his taint until he found that magic spot that made Drake moan.

"Fuck, Garrett, feels so good," Drake managed.

Garrett reached for the lube he had already stashed nearby and slicked up his right hand, gripping the base of Drake's cock with his left. He nudged Drake until he fell onto his back, and his legs splayed wide, still keeping up a rhythm with his mouth.

"Damn—you've been reading those books? God, don't stop."

Garrett eased one slippery finger into Drake's hole, making him buck with the gentle intrusion. He slipped it in and out in time with how his mouth worked Drake's cock, knowing it wasn't going to take much more to make him come.

"I'm real close," Drake breathed. "Last chance to pull off."

Instead, Garrett added another finger in Drake's ass and swirled his tongue across the head and through the slit of his cock, then pressed against the sensitive spot just under the flare. Drake arched and came, and Garrett did his best to swallow it all.

He pulled off with a pop. While Drake lay pliant and blissed out, Garrett pushed his knees up and withdrew the fingers, only to push his face into the cleft of Drake's ass and replace fingers with his tongue.

"Oh, fuck," was all Drake could manage as Garrett began

working him with both his tongue and fingers, adding a third and curling them to stroke Drake's prostate. He had already experimented on his own ass, finding that magic spot and figuring out what felt good.

Drake's hands clenched the sheets as Garrett continued to lick and stroke, getting Drake's hole loose and wet. He climbed up between Drake's legs, with his rock-hard cock and heavy balls making his need clear.

"Okay if I fuck you?" Garrett hoped he sounded more seductive than nervous.

"Think I'll die of frustration if you don't," Drake gasped.

Garrett gripped Drake's hips and lined himself up, pressing in slowly so he didn't hurt his lover. No matter how much he had read or how many videos he watched, this was still new to him, and he wanted to get it right.

"It's good. So good. Just go with it," Drake begged.

Garrett pushed all the way until he was fully seated and looked into Drake's eyes. "Like you on your back when we do this. Want to see your face."

"Please...move."

Garrett slid out and back, slowly at first, then setting up a rhythm and making sure he nailed Drake's prostate every few strokes. He kept going until Drake began to harden again. His cock hadn't gotten the message about slower second rounds.

"Love you so much," Garrett whispered, hoping he left fingerprints on Drake's hips. "Want to make this good for you."

"Oh...it's definitely...good," Drake managed. "Love you too."

Garrett felt his orgasm rising and quickened his pace, wondering if Drake would feel him when he walked tomorrow. He pounded his way through his climax, only slowing down when the crest waned. Garrett withdrew carefully, knowing Drake's hole would be tender.

"That was…" Drake said.

"Not done." Garrett shifted forward until his ass was above Drake's stiffening cock, and he let himself down in one move until the whole shaft disappeared.

Drake yelped with surprise. "Don't hurt yourself."

Garrett chuckled. "Had a plug in all afternoon. Nice and open and slick for you."

Drake's head dropped back onto the pillow. "You're going to kill me."

"There are worse ways to go."

Garrett's thighs were already beginning to burn, and he knew he couldn't ride Drake for long, but despite Drake's disclaimer, his cock plumped up in record time, and Garrett wrung a second climax from both of them.

"How did you…get all that out of those books?" Drake finally said when he had caught his breath. They lay together, sweaty, sticky, and completely fucked out.

"Always been a straight-A student," Garrett laughed. "That was the *only* thing straight about me."

"We should probably take a shower and change the sheets before we're stuck here," Drake said after they lay bonelessly still for a while.

"Probably. Think we can get round three in the shower?" Garrett grinned. "I'm up for trying."

"You're incorrigible."

"Oh, for you, I'm totally corrigible."

"That's not a word."

"It is now."

"Okay, as long as we can be corrigible together." Drake pressed a kiss to Garrett's head.

"Always."

AFTERWORD

Thank you for following the Carnival of Mysteries series, Season 2! If you haven't already read Season 1, you're in for a real treat—including my book, *Roustabout*.

Drake first appeared in *Signs and Wonders* in my Witch-bane series, where he helped Seth and Evan shut down the dark witch whose absence causes all kinds of problems as the survivors fight for territory.

Eagle-eyed readers will catch some other oblique references to other characters and other books. I love leaving little Easter eggs for readers!

All my Morgan Brice series cross over with each other—and with the modern-day Gail Z. Martin and Gail Z. Martin/Larry N. Martin books. It's much more fun that way and a whole lot less for me to keep straight!

ACKNOWLEDGMENTS

It really does take a village to bring a book to life. Thank you to all my beta and ARC readers, to my amazing editor, Misty Massey, and to my husband, Larry N. Martin who works so hard behind the scenes to get the books into final form. I couldn't make this happen without you.

Thanks also to the bloggers, assistants, and promotional partners who help spread the word so people know the books exist. I appreciate everything you do.

Most of all, thanks to my wonderful readers, who enjoy visiting and re-visiting the supernatural worlds I write about. You make it all worthwhile. Because you read, I write.

ABOUT THE AUTHOR

Morgan Brice is the romance pen name of bestselling author Gail Z. Martin. Morgan writes urban fantasy male/male paranormal romance, with plenty of action, adventure, and supernatural thrills to go with the happily ever after.

Gail writes epic fantasy and urban fantasy, and together with co-author hubby Larry N. Martin, steampunk and comedic horror, all of which have less romance and more explosions.

On the rare occasions Morgan isn't writing, she's either reading, cooking, or spoiling two very pampered dogs.

Watch for additional new series from Morgan Brice and more books in the Witchbane, Badlands, Treasure Trail, Kings of the Mountain, Sharps & Springfield, and Fox Hollow universes coming soon!

Where to find me, and how to stay in touch

Join my Worlds of Morgan Brice Facebook Group and get in on all the behind-the-scenes fun! My free reader group is the first to see cover reveals, learn tidbits about works-in-progress, have fun with exclusive contests and giveaways, find out about in-person get-togethers, and more! It's also where I find my beta readers, ARC readers, and launch team! Come join the party! https://www.Facebook.com/groups/WorldsOfMorganBrice

Find me on the web at https://morganbrice.com. You can also find me on Twitter/X: @MorganBriceBook, on Pinterest (for Morgan and Gail): pinterest.com/Gzmartin, on

Instagram as MorganBriceAuthor, on YouTube at https://www.youtube.com/c/GailZMartinAuthor/ on Bookbub https://www.bookbub.com/authors/morgan-brice and on TikTok @MorganBriceAuthor

Check out the ongoing, online convention ConTinual www.facebook.com/groups/ConTinual

Support Indie Authors

When you support independent authors, you help influence what kind of books you'll see and what types of stories will be available because the authors themselves decide what to write, not a big publishing conglomerate. Independent authors are local creators supporting their families with the books they produce. Thank you for supporting independent authors and small press fiction!

Gruff

Trash and Treasure

A Taste of Danger: Subparheroes

Kings of the Mountain Series

Kings of the Mountain

The Christmas Spirit, a Kings of the Mountain Short Story

Sins of the Fathers

Kings of the Mountain Universe

Roustabout : Carnival of Mysteries

Sharps & Springfield Series

Peacemaker

Treasure Trail Series

Treasure Trail

Blink

Last Resort

Secrets and Ciphers, a Treasure Trail Novella

Treasure Trail Universe

Light My Way Home, a Treasure Trail Short Story

Witchbane Series

Witchbane

Burn, a Witchbane Novella

Dark Rivers

Flame and Ash

Unholy

The Devil You Know

Signs and Wonders

The Christmas Crunch, a Witchbane Short Story

Sandwiched, a Witchbane Short Story

Ambushed, A Witchbane Novella

Midnight on the Midway: Carnival of Mysteries

Castle Magic: A Caynham Castle Collection

CARNIVAL OF MYSTERIES

Once more we bid you Welcome, Travelers, to Errante Ame's Carnival of Mysteries! Join us for another round of fantastic, space-and-time spanning tales by a talented group of some of the best authors to be found in M/M romance. Whether you enjoy mystery, action, danger, or just sweet romance, there is something for everyone at the Carnival!